LABYRINTH OF THE LOST
AND OTHER MACABRE CRIME STORIES

ALSO BY EDMUND GLASBY

Disciple of a Dark God (2010)
Re-worked as a trilogy:
Disciple of a Dark God, The Hand of Cyrvilus,
and *An Unholy Crusade* (all 2018)
The Dyrysgol Horror* (2012)
The Ash Murders* (2013)
The Chaos of Chung-Fu* (2013)
Dark Shadows* (2014)
Ghouls of the Undercity* (2014)
The Weird Shadow Over Morecambe* (2014)
A Murder Most Macabre (2015)
Death After Death (2016)
The Doppelganger Deaths (2016)
The Postbox Murders (2016)
Where Blood Runs Deep (2016)
Angels of Death* (2017)
Screamworld (2018)
Wraith of Vengeance (2019)
A Hundred Thousand Reasons for Revenge (2019)

(*Available in Wildside editions)

LABYRINTH OF THE LOST
AND OTHER MACABRE CRIME STORIES

WILDSIDE PRESS

Published by Wildside Press LLC.
wildsidepress.com | bcmystery.com

CONTENTS

CONTENTS

INTRODUCTION

I have long had a fascination with horror and supernatural fiction—interests no doubt stemming from the fact that my father, John S. Glasby, was a prolific author who particularly enjoyed writing in these genres. As well as pursuing a successful scientific career in the fields of industrial chemistry and astronomy he wrote consistently from the early 1950s right up to his death in 2011. He first turned his hand to writing science fiction novels and his initial stories were published in 1952 by Curtis Warren under the pen names of Rand Le Page, Berl Cameron and Paul Lorraine. In 1954 John Spencer Ltd. commissioned him to write short stories with a supernatural theme for the new pocket book series, Supernatural Stories. This series proved to be popular and continued until 1967, with my father contributing over one hundred stories under a plethora of pseudonyms.

My father had been a great fan of Howard Phillips Lovecraft who had created a set of hugely influential horror stories based on aeons-old alien gods and their malign activities on this planet—the so-called Cthulhu Mythos. Lovecraftian concepts had peppered some of his earlier stories and from the 1970s he was able to focus on developing these themes and had a collection accepted by August Derleth which would have been released in 1972. Unfortunately Derleth passed away before this came to fruition. According to John Pelan, my father was the first British author to write Lovecraftian fiction.

I grew up with these influences yet at the same time was not fully aware of my father's considerable writing achievements. As I was born in December 1970 it was not until the mid to late 1980s that I began to read his works and truly appreciate them. The Supernatural Stories of the 1950s and 1960s had completely passed me by and I only really discovered them after his death. These stories, while a little dated at times, have great imagination, atmosphere and originality and it was when I took it upon myself to seek them out for posterity (and possible re-publication) that the idea of writing stories in a similar vein occurred to me. I had already written an epic dark fantasy story, Disciple of a Dark God just after completing my academic studies at the University of Oxford. Writing short stories provided a different challenge that I enjoyed. It gave me the opportunity to explore many diverse themes that drew on all the things that had influenced me; from my father's work and all the fantasy and horror films I loved in the 1980s to my interests in world mythologies and my studies in Anthropology and Egyptian Archaeology.

The inspiration for the short stories collected here are gathered from all those sources and from a lifelong habit of people-watching. I will admit to a certain fascination with 'strange' characters. Ideas for stories evolve from various situations and 'what if' scenarios.

The title story, Labyrinth of the Lost starts from the premise of how to identify a suspected murder victim when all that is found is a severed arm.

In Curse of the Dead I wanted to write a dynamic horror story exploring a variation on the living dead. Originally titled Nyongo, I got the idea for this one from a lecture I sat in on concerning various African superstitions and occult practices.

For The Resurrection of Nicholas Zegrembi I returned to one of my father's creations. Nicholas Zegrembi had been referenced in a couple of his Supernatural Stories and I felt deserved another lease of life, or something approximating life…

The belief in past life regression is a central theme in Death After Death, which explores the terrors that could occur if someone malign were able to gain access to an individual's past. This is a gruesome tale where a man is apparently haunted by his previous self.

The relatively recent phenomena of live action role playing (larping) provided a good starting point for stranding strangers in a remote setting, where things suddenly turn for the worse. Such is the case in The Madness of Morgenstein.

All five stories in this collection are completely different but share an appreciation for fast-paced, fantastical escapist fiction with a large dollop of Grand Guignol horror.

—Edmund Glasby
July 2020

LABYRINTH OF THE LOST

Once branded…forever damned.

"Believe me, Henry, it's astounding!" Kieran Miller was gesticulating enthusiastically with his fork, the food before him forgotten in his excitement. "Absolutely amazing!"

"I'm glad you approve of the new prototype system. I had wondered if you might have had a problem adapting to it." Detective Inspector Henry Garford regarded Miller with amused affection. They had met for lunch in the station canteen as they did most Thursdays and Miller, a top fingerprint expert and forensic specialist, had not stopped enthusing about the planned computerisation of fingerprint analysis throughout the whole meal.

"Admittedly, at first I was a little sceptical about it and I still think you can't beat a trained pair of eyes, but the speed of it—I've run test after test and the margin of error is virtually zero, even when it's comparing thousands of prints." Miller sighed happily. "It's going to completely revolutionise my craft, believe me. The amount of evidential data that can be stored, assimilated and analysed is quite literally out of this world."

"Perhaps it'll give you more time for research?" Garford suggested with a questioning smile.

"You bet!" Miller beamed. He had worked for the police for over twenty years and was passionate about his job, particularly the most difficult cases where he had to piece together prints from fragments. In the small amount of quiet time that a lull in work sometimes granted he had pushed fingerprint techniques as far as he could. A year before, he had worked on identifying leather and rubber gloves from traces they left behind. Garford had laughed at this research until the day it had secured a conviction for him. It was slightly doubtful whether the evidence would have stood up in court on its own merits but after the defendant had admitted that the slightly worn gloves were his own and Miller had presented the enlarged photographs of the marks found at the crime scene, there had been a change of plea to guilty. Since then, the station had joked that Miller could find prints on anything from a tea towel to a puff of smoke.

"So what's your latest project then?" Garford asked, grimacing as his coffee proved to be even worse than usual.

"Cold cases," Miller replied. "Many of which have lain unsolved and forgotten for years, decades even. There are a lot that I've been wanting to re-check—the worst of the ones that foxed even me. With the computer to check my work I might get somewhere at last."

Garford pushed himself to his feet. "Well don't forget to go home occasionally. Last thing I need is your missus giving me grief for overworking you. I know what you're like, Kieran Miller, when you get the bit between your teeth. As tenacious as a bloody bulldog."

* * * *

The sun filtered through the canopy of leaves and the soft breeze carried the scents of pine trees and flowers. The beauty and peace of the scene was, however, marred by the severed arm with its shining knob of slightly protruding bone and attached lump of pink-red gristle, lying beside a tree.

Garford regarded the sunny glade with a slight sense of excitement. He loved solving mysteries, always had, and this looked like the beginning of a good one. The fact that there was only an arm at this stage made it easier of course, the victim of this crime did not yet exist for him as a personality. His attitude would change later, as it always did, when he got to know the victim—whether it was a criminal who had pushed his luck too far, or an innocent who needed justice to be done for them. That was, of course, assuming that the owner of the arm was indeed dead.

Eyes down, walking carefully over the grass, Garford noted the lack of blood or any real disturbance of the earth. The first conclusion his detective mind suggested to him was that the limb had not been severed here. Turning his attention to the arm itself, he guessed that it was that of a middle-aged man, No rings, no tattoos, no scars, white-skinned with a faint tan from the elbow down. If they were really lucky, he thought, the man's prints might be on their files, enabling identification, but that was a long shot. From what he could see, the arm had been hacked off, none too neatly, just below the shoulder.

Surely unless that had been done by a surgeon, the man would have bled to death, if of course he was still alive when the procedure had begun.

They had had a bit of luck with the discovery of the arm. Sergeant Grant had found it on his way to work. The small glade felt somewhat separate but it was part of a popular footpath to the town centre and they could be reasonably certain that the arm had not been there the previous afternoon or someone would surely have reported it.

After a few minutes, Miller and his assistant Scene of Crime Officer appeared, carrying their bags of equipment. With a cheerful nod to Garford, Miller set about examining the arm and the area.

"I wonder where the rest of him is?" said Garford, watching with some interest as the two forensic scientists went about their business.

"Impossible to say," Miller replied, examining the hand with a magnifying glass. He frowned, confusedly. "Hmm. Well, that's odd."

"What is?" Garford took a step forward, curious.

With the aid of the magnifying glass, Miller peered, scrutinising the thumb. "There's what appears to be an elliptic design on the pad. There are a series of thin lines within it. It looks like a maze. It *might* be keloidic or hypertrophic scarification." He shook his head bemusedly. "No, maybe not. I'd say it's a—"

"A tattoo?"

"No. I'd say this was a brand."

"You mean it was *burnt* on?"

"Looks like it. Obviously, I'll know more when we get it back to the laboratory."

Secure in the knowledge that Miller would leave no stone unturned, Garford decided to return to the station and set in motion the usual routes of enquiry. An hour later, he knew that no one had been admitted to hospital locally with a missing arm and no armless bodies had been reported. Until more information came to light he could only speculate about the explanation. At about two o'clock, Garford wandered down to the basement where Miller worked.

"Do you have anything for me, Kieran?" he asked, not very hopefully.

Miller was peering intently at the screen of his computer, the green glow reflecting on his perplexed face. "Well, actually, I think I have." He paused, cross-referencing the data on the screen with a finger. "At least, I might."

Garford pulled up a chair and sat down next to him.

"Well, it was easy enough getting a good clear set of prints for the arm and it does match someone on our files."

"Brilliant! I had no idea the computer was that quick!" Garford exclaimed.

"It's not. I recognised the print myself."

"What! You can't possibly remember every print you've taken!"

"Of course not, Henry. It's the mark on the thumb. I remembered this print, well you would wouldn't you? I've often wondered what it was meant to signify." Miller gestured to the computer. "I confirmed the match with this and it's definite. The prints belong to Albert Fielding, fifty-four, convicted of burglary three years ago and sentenced to four and half years."

"He must have been granted parole. Great work. I'll find out what he did on leaving prison." Garford got up to leave.

"That's the problem, Henry. I've already checked—he's still in jail."

* * * *

Following a long conversation with the prison authorities, Garford had confirmed that Fielding was indeed still incarcerated and in possession of all his limbs including a right hand with a strange thumb mark. There had to be a mistake in the records. Miller would have to go to the prison and take his prints again for the files. However, the fact remained that Fielding seemed to have a mark that was at least strikingly similar to the one they had found and even if he was not the victim, he might know something of interest.

Garford had visited prisons on occasion during his career but he never got over the feeling of claustrophobia that attended his visits. It was Miller's first time, however, and he seemed to be interested rather than oppressed by the experience. After their credentials had been checked they were shown to a small room with chairs and a table where Miller set up his ink pad and cards.

"Do you think there's been an error somewhere along the line?" queried Garford.

"Possibly. But I really don't know how we can have got the records mixed up. There are good protocols in place to prevent mistakes of that kind."

"Unlikely as it may seem, I suppose there must be someone else we've arrested in the past who had the same mark on their thumb and it was assumed to be unique and got misfiled," Garford speculated.

"Could be some kind of gang symbol, I agree, but the other digits would be different—it should not have happened."

After a few minutes, the door opened and a prison guard brought in a slightly chubby, middle-aged man—Albert Fielding.

"What's all this about then? The parole hearing isn't due for six months." Noticing the fingerprinting tools, he added: "That's all been done before you know. Along with my mugshot, you did my fingers and thumbs before I came in here, remember?"

"Mr. Fielding, we would like to take a copy of your fingerprints as there may be an anomaly in our records." Garford waved the man towards the waiting chair.

"What? I've nearly served my time. I've been doing porridge in here for three years, so don't you go trying to fit anything new me," Fielding said defensively. He gulped nervously. It would be just like this lot to frame him for something he didn't do just to keep him inside.

"There's no question of that, I can assure you," replied Garford.

"Yeah, and you expect me to believe that? Ah well, hurry it up and let's get it done. I've got to get back to staring at my cell walls."

Miller swiftly inked and printed, checking that he had a clear set. "These should be fine. Thank you for your cooperation."

Garford looked at the thumbprint on the right hand. It was definitely a maze, highlighted more clearly with the ink. "What can you tell me about this design?" he asked.

"The labyrinth?" Fielding looked surprised. "It doesn't mean anything. It's just a—well, I suppose it was a dare."

"A dare?" Garford asked, raising his eyebrows. "Tell me about it."

"Why should I?"

"Because I'm asking and you'll want to stay on my good side, what with your parole coming up soon. Me and the Governor are like that." Garford crossed his fingers.

"Very well. It was years ago so I don't see any harm. When I was about twenty, I hung around with quite a few people who were a bit dodgy—nothing extreme; a bit of theft, mostly from warehouses, that sort of thing. Learnt a lot of stuff from them…more's the pity." He added hastily: "Some of them had tattoos and wanted us all to get one, like a gang thing, you know? I was up for that but then one of the lads—Johnnie Walker—"

"Surely that wasn't his real name!" Miller interjected with a snort.

"Nah, he was Johnnie something or other, but where we all drank beer, he loved his whisky, so he got that nickname. Well, he said we should be different, cooler. He had an idea that we should brand ourselves." He smiled wryly at the memory. "Even for a bunch of hard lads like we thought we were, that sounded a bit stupid. Johnnie went on and on about it though, and he was forever doodling on things, trying out designs. One day he asked us all to meet down our local boozer as he had heard of a really good job someone wanted doing. We all turned up and Johnnie took us to an old building that hadn't been lived in for years. He had set up a table and some chairs and got some beers in but he had also put a drawing of a maze on the table— quite a big one. Some of the lads started to laugh and make jokes about having to steal a minotaur but Johnnie just waited for them to stop. After a bit he said that this job was a proper heist; serious money if we pulled it off and serious respect from the people that mattered. But there was a catch—always is, isn't there? Johnnie wouldn't tell us anymore about it unless we agreed to his branding plan. As you can imagine there was a bit of argy bargy after that but Johnnie ended all the arguing." Fielding chuckled. "He took a great chunk of gold out of his pocket, a big bloody nugget—the kind of thing you see only in comics—and slammed it down on the table and said: 'You can all get your hands on some of these—if you're brave enough—and I want proof that you won't bottle out and you won't welch.'"

"Are you sure it was really gold?" Miller asked sceptically.

"Definite. There's a heaviness and a feel to gold, solid gold, that you get to recognise, and he wasn't lying."

"So presumably you all agreed to Johnnie's conditions?" Garford asked.

"You bet we did! None of us were going to pass up on that kind of wealth. We got the mark just like he wanted and swore not to tell anyone about the job. Hurt like hell for a while, but I admit I've grown to like it." Fielding absently rubbed his thumb and forefinger together.

"What did the job turn out to be?" Garford asked curiously.

Fielding held up his thumb. "Don't welch, remember?" he answered, grinning.

Garford resisted his policeman's urge to know. He had a more pressing question at the moment. "Can you remember who else got this brand?"

Fielding gave him a calculating look. "How about you tell me why you're asking?"

"I've no problem with that. A man's severed arm was discovered yesterday and the only identifying feature was his fingerprints, including a maze design on his thumb." He omitted to say that the prints on the hand had come up as Fielding's.

"Christ! It could well be one of the lads! I've never met anyone else with it. Just an arm you say?"

"Yes, so if you can give me some names…I'm sure it would be beneficial to your parole hearing." Garford took out his notebook to record the list of names that rattled out of Fielding's mouth.

* * * *

The insistent ringing of the telephone made Garford throw on his dressing gown and dash down the stairs, his hair still wet from the shower. He made it to the phone just in time. "Yes?" he said rather breathlessly.

"Henry, finally! They said you had gone home." It was Miller.

"Well, I do, occasionally," Garford replied dryly.

"It's the prints—Fielding's prints."

"What about them?"

"They still match the arm!"

"What?"

"They still match. Fielding's prints that I took today, exactly match those of the arm. I've checked it over and over. There's no doubt about it."

Garford rubbed his free hand through his hair. "Twins?" he suggested.

"Nothing doing. Even identical twins have different prints."

"Then, how on earth…?"

"I've no idea, Henry. I've been trying to think of possible explanations until my head feels like there's a thunderstorm in it."

"There has to be something we've missed—unless you're the first man to discover a double in prints. You'll be famous."

"Very funny, but do you really think that the infinitesimal chance of an exact double which is about one-in-sixty-four billion, would also match up with the extremely slim chance of someone getting exactly the same brand? Even if one were to take every human being that has ever existed on the planet I doubt you'd ever get as positive a match as this." Miller sounded almost hysterical. "I just don't understand it."

"I admit it's a mystery at the moment. Why don't you go home now and we'll meet up in the morning."

"But I can't...I've got to get back to it. This is so bloody intriguing. I'll get back in touch if I discover anything else."

"Okay, but don't overdo it."

Putting the phone down, Garford reflected that it really was an interesting mystery. He dismissed the possibility that Miller had been mistaken—he knew him too well. Garford pottered about the house on automatic, making tea, checking the post and turning on the gas fire in the living room. His wife, Sally, would be back soon, hopefully. His irregular hours were often trumped by hers as a district nurse. The puzzle of the arm was a tricky one to be sure but he might get a lead from the names Fielding had given him. Sipping his tea in the living room, his eyes fell on the bottle of whisky in a glass-fronted cabinet alongside a rather old bottle of sherry. The one person he would really like to find was Johnnie Walker. Garford had a feeling that he was a cut above the likes of Fielding in intelligence and that all that business with the brand was more than a little worrying. Yes, he nodded to himself, a little talk with Johnnie Walker was definitely in order but in the meantime he'd have a sip of his namesake.

* * * *

Garford's planned meeting with Miller the following morning was not to be. The moment he entered the station he had to deal with a report that had come in from the prison. Albert Fielding had been found dead in his cell.

"Was it suicide or natural causes?" Garford asked the Governor on the phone

Surely murder was out of the question. It wasn't as though Fielding was incarcerated one of the high-security prisons that had a reputation for lawlessness.

"To be honest, I don't see how it can have been either. It looks like he may've bled to death. The floor was awash with it. You see, his right arm had been cut off."

"*What?* What did you say?" Garford felt his throat constrict, contorting his voice slightly. His head spun.

"His cell was locked when the warden did his rounds. There were no blades of any kind, but Fielding's arm was on the floor beside the bed. The rest of him was still on the bed and he looked like he had just fallen asleep, no sign of a struggle. Does the reason you came to see him yesterday have any bearing on this?" asked the Governor.

Garford hesitated. It was too much of a coincidence not to be connected but he was damned if he could see what it all meant. "I'd better come and see him. I'll be right over." He rang off and set to gathering a team to take to the prison. He debated briefly whether to take Miller. He had sounded slightly hysterical yesterday. However, he was the station's best man and any deaths in custody had to be investigated scrupulously or the press would have a field day. They were going to be all over this anyway, the obvious solution was that a prison officer had either killed Fielding or at least colluded in his murder. No, he had to bring Miller. Thinking about the 'obvious solution', could it be that Fielding had told people about the discovered arm, an unwise and ultimately fatal decision that could that have sparked off a kind of copycat murder? Garford shook himself mentally. It was no good speculating too much yet, they had to gather evidence first.

To his relief, Miller was in a better frame of mind that morning. As they drove to the prison he told Garford that he had contacted a colleague in Derby. "If you authorise it he's happy to come and check my work, it's just possible I'm wrong," he had said, openly admitting his own fallibility—something he very rarely did.

At the prison they went straight to Fielding's cell. The corpse and everything else was still in situ. Nothing had been touched after it had been confirmed that Fielding was beyond saving. The pool of blood had congealed but not dried and the bed was badly stained. Fielding himself, though deathly white, looked perfectly peaceful.

"Drugged, I suppose," Miller suggested. "He must have been alive when the arm was removed or there would not have been so much blood. The heart must have continued pumping for quite a while to cause all this. I'll check for all the usual possibilities but it certainly looks like he died through blood loss."

"What about the arm? How do you think it was removed?" Garford asked.

"Well, it's a reasonably clean cut but not perfect. There's some evidence that a second blow was required. I would think a meat cleaver or similar weapon could do it. Maybe a wood axe." Miller set his assistant to photographing the body and the room while he unpacked the rest of the equipment. "I'll be here some time. There's a lot to go over. Obviously I'll dust the door handle and other surfaces and we'll need to do the usual elimination screening."

"Right. I'll leave you to it. I think I've seen all I need to here at the moment. Time to talk to the Governor." Garford left, glad to be away from the strong, cloying smell of blood.

The interview with the Governor was a little difficult. It seemed to him that their visit the previous day must have been the catalyst for Fielding]s murder and Garford had to agree.

"As things stand, the only clue I have is that Fielding gave me a list of names yesterday and he's now dead, in a very strange manner. I'm following up those names today but can you tell me if any of them are familiar to you, either as inmates or staff. Take a look will you?" He handed over the list.

After a few moments, the Governor looked up. "No, I don't recognise these, but I can check if one of them is here. If so, and he'd heard about the blabbing, he may have believed he'd been betrayed by Fielding. That then provides a motive, but it doesn't explain how it was done. Despite the fact that Fielding was on the 'good behaviour' wing we still maintain a stringent security here. His cell was locked, with a prison officer sat at the end of the corridor. Nor does it explain the arm you discovered prior to this. Hell, we don't even have a murder weapon as yet."

Garford sighed. "I like a challenge, but this is in a different league. I'm going to need to interview all your officers and anyone who had access to Fielding yesterday."

"You can use one of the interview rooms to take statements. I don't think that any of my officers would be party to such a brutal crime so the sooner you can clear them the better."

Garford wished it was that simple.

* * * *

Daniel Cooper had been feeling ill all morning, slightly sick and with a growing headache. The rather stuffy office he worked in wasn't helping and at two o'clock in the afternoon he decided enough was enough. No point in being the boss if you can't knock off early, he thought to himself as he drove out of the car park. Five minutes into the journey, Cooper felt himself drifting into unconsciousness and only just managed to verge the car before a pulse of pressure blossomed behind his eyes and his brain died.

* * * *

Garford read the attending officer's report with a mixture of excitement and frustration. Local businessman found dead of an apparent cerebral aneurism. No witnesses. No suspicion of foul play, but when the officer had checked for a pulse he had seen the peculiar mark of a maze on the man's thumb.

Sure enough, the name Daniel Cooper had been on Fielding's list. Their research had turned up six of the original gang still alive and, coincidentally, he had been going to contact Cooper that very day. He had phoned one other, Keith Southgate, but had only established that he was now a bricklayer and had not been in touch with any of the others for years. The darts team he was in had been playing last night and at least a dozen people could give him an alibi. Of Johnnie Walker, Southgate would only say: "He was the smart one, never really the leader but we seemed to end up doing what he wanted anyway. He could be a bit strange if you didn't do as he said."

* * * *

Miller looked once again at Cooper's fingerprints, including the branded thumb. To his relief, they were different from Fielding's, although he felt sure the mark had been made by the same brand. A little knot of tension in his stomach that he had been unaware of slowly dissipated. A few feet away from him sat Richard Latham, his colleague from Derby, who was meticulously going over the prints of Fielding and of the severed arm. Hopefully he would be able to throw some light on the problem. At length, Latham sat back from the desk and pushed his glasses up onto his head.

"Kieran, I'm afraid that your eyes are as good as ever. These are as identical a pair of prints as I've ever seen."

Miller felt his heart sink. "But, how can that be? You know as well as I do that it's virtually impossible. The odds against it are astronomical."

"Well, every rule has an exception." Latham gave an unconvincing smile but he looked worried. "Actually, I've heard of something similar to this. It's one of the reasons why I wanted to help you."

"Go on." Intrigued, Miller nodded.

"You remember Professor Marianne Verner? She's working in Edinburgh these days. We met at a conference last year and she told me about a case she'd been unable to solve. A body had been discovered in a lake—a loch, I suppose they call them up there. It had been there for a least a week and was quite badly decomposed or rather eaten, nibbled away at by fish, eels, otters and Christ knows what else. No prints, as there was too much damage to the hands, but the skull and teeth were all intact. So far it was just a puzzle as to who he was and why he was dead in a loch. However, the forensic team working on the body were struck by the similarity to another cadaver in their morgue. This was a recently deceased man, I can't remember his name, who had collapsed in the process of breaking into a house. Verner put the two bodies side by side and, even allowing for the state of the decomposition of the loch body, she deduced that, anatomically, they could have been twins. The only real difference was that the one they pulled out of the loch had no recent dental work but the old fillings exactly matched the oldest fillings of the burglar. He just had extra, later ones as well. It was as if the two had experienced exactly the same problems up to a certain point and then their lives had diverged."

"That sounds bizarre! Incredible," Miller exclaimed. "And the explanation?"

"There never was one." Latham shook his head. "The burglar, who had been an only child, was deemed to have died of natural causes and his body was released to his family for burial. The other corpse was never identified and was eventually buried as a John Doe." Latham pulled his glasses back down onto the bridge of his nose. He picked up the print of Fielding's thumb and looked at it for a moment before clearing his throat to speak. "Another thing I remembered is that Verner mentioned that the burglar's body had been quite heavily decorated; scarified, lots of tribal tattoos and even marks that had been burnt in…"

Miller and Latham looked at each other worriedly then Miller broke the silence. "We need to tell Garford."

As Miller and Latham entered Garford's office, the Detective Inspector had just ended a telephone call. He put the receiver down and extended his hand. "I'm pleased to meet you, Mr. Latham. Do you have any ideas about our conundrum?"

"I don't know if I'm helping the case or making it murkier," Latham said, shaking hands. He explained about Marianne Verner's experience.

"Can you get in touch with her and ask if there was any mark on his right thumb? We could well have a serial killer here. I've just been talking to a Tony March, one of those on the list, who thinks he knows where Johnnie Walker might be these days. He said Walker was an odd one, liked to be 'pulling the strings' were his words. Apparently, Walker leads a fairly nomadic life but usually turns up in town every few months. He's still into theft and seems to like recruiting a new team each time. March caught sight of him last week and gave me a possible address. I got the impression there's no love lost between the two. In addition, he also knows the man's real name. John Carrion."

"What does this Tony March do now?" Miller asked curiously. "The name sounds familiar."

"Believe it or not, he's a wrestler—quite a good one, or so I've heard. You've probably seen his name on a poster." Garford rose to his feet, feeling more positive about the case now. "You call your contact about her dead burglar. Get as much as you can from her, no matter how seemingly irrelevant. I'll get Hatton to accompany me to see if we can track down Carrion."

* * * *

The unmarked car pulled into a side street in a slightly run-down part of the town. Miller had radioed through a message to say Verner had confirmed that the burglar had indeed been the bearer of a labyrinth brand on his right thumb. The name had not matched any that Fielding had given them but he could have forgotten someone or the man could have changed his name.

Garford knocked on the door of a rather nondescript house and stepped back, watching to see if anyone peered out of the windows. A minute later, the door opened. Garford was not sure what he had been expecting—a tough guy, a spiv or a weasel—but what he got was a slim, tanned, alert-looking man. His clothes were casual but of good quality and he looked fit for his age which must been somewhere in the early fifties. He had intense, piercing blue eyes.

"Yes?" the man said, enquiringly.

"I'm Detective Inspector Garford and this is Sergeant Hatton. Are you Mr. John Carrion?"

"I am indeed. How can I help you?" Carrion replied calmly.

"Mr. Carrion, I'm investigating several deaths which seem to be linked to a gang you were part of many years ago."

"*A gang?* I've never been part of a gang." Carrion looked partly amused and partly annoyed.

"May I see your hands?" Garford asked abruptly, watching him intently.

Something definitely changed in Carrion's eyes and he paused briefly before giving a slight shrug of acquiescence. "I suppose so. Although it's a rather unusual request." He extended both hands, palm down.

Garford turned them over and noted the familiar design on the thumb. "I'd like to know the significance of this mark."

"If you like, but why don't you come inside. It's a long story." Carrion stepped aside to let them past.

The living room was neatly furnished but completely lacking in personality. Probably rented, Garford guessed.

"Who has named me as a gang member, may I ask?"

"Some people who mostly remember you as Johnnie Walker," Garford replied, hoping for a reaction.

Carrion said nothing for a moment, then looked directly at Garford with a smile. "Well, well. Now that's interesting." He rose quickly to his feet and Garford felt himself tense up, the sergeant who had stayed standing in the doorway of the room was also on the alert but Carrion merely opened a cabinet and took out a bottle of whisky and a glass. "Can I offer you a drink? No, then I will have a small one myself." He poured himself a generous measure and sat back down again. "The story of the labyrinth." He took a sip and started to talk. "I was never part of a gang, although I've known a few in my time. I've no need to be part of a crowd."

"Albert Fielding and Tony March say otherwise," Garford interrupted.

"Bert and Tony! Names from the past indeed. They probably thought I *was* in their gang, to be honest. No, I'm definitely a lone wolf, but if you want to find a collection of men of a certain kind, criminality is a good bet. You see, I knew if I could get together twenty or so strong young men there would be considerable profit in it for me."

"This mysterious job that they won't talk about, even now? The one they were paid in gold for?" asked Garford.

"They *still* won't talk? That is gratifying. Pointless, but gratifying." Carrion rose and started to pace slowly round the room, swirling his drink. "That was my first shipment and paved the way for a very lucrative career." He paused and turned to the sergeant. "Why don't you sit down?"

The young man immediately sank to the floor, his eyes glazed. Garford tried to move to assist him but found his muscles would not work. "What are you doing, Carrion?" he asked with an effort.

Carrion smiled pleasantly at him. "Getting your undivided attention. How did you come to be involved in this anyway?"

Garford could just about talk but his tongue felt heavy and clumsy. "We found...an arm."

"Oh, yes, I missed that one."

"And a body...in Scotland."

"That must have been Smithy, I thought he would have decomposed sooner." Carrion came close to Garford and looked into his eyes as if assessing something. "Would you like to know *everything* inspector?" he whispered. His words now dripped like acid.

Garford could no longer move his mouth and was desperately hoping that something would happen to get them out of there. He had no doubts that Carrion had somehow drugged them and intended to kill them. How, he did not know. They had not eaten or drunk anything. Perhaps there was some kind of gas in the air, but if so why was Carrion unaffected?

"When I was a lot younger, I wanted money, lots of it and I wasn't too worried how I got it. I got to know all the dodges but it was still small stuff until the day I broke into a particular house. The moment I climbed in the window, I knew it was special, dangerous. There were things there I had never seen before, powerful things, and I wanted them." Carrion's eyes gleamed at the memory. "I knew I could just take them, but I wanted to know more, to learn more, so I searched the house from top to bottom. The owner might come back at any time and I wanted to be ready with my offer. When he returned, I had decided what to do. I waited in the living room, if you can call it that, and made my proposal. I would do anything at all if he would teach me about the magic—I suppose you would call it black magic—that I could feel all around. He regarded me for a long moment and I knew that he could have killed me instantly, but I stood my ground. Eventually, he laughed and said that there was a career opportunity for someone like me, if I was serious." He began pacing again, sipping his drink.

Garford could see that the other was not walking aimlessly, rather he was deliberately following a pattern, turning regularly. The room seemed to be changing, growing bigger and darker as he walked. A mystical sigil began to appear on the carpet.

"I was serious all right. I could feel the power he had and I wanted it, or at least a share. My master, for such he became, wanted workers of a sort, but genuine recruits were hard to come by. He wanted a way to bring in more than one at a time and as we talked I came up with the solution. How to get the right kind of people to sell away their humanity—their souls—and become slaves. The job I invented was merely a lure and Fielding, March, Smithy, all of them took the bait. When they accepted the brand they became His. As I walked them over the threshold of the abandoned factory they went from this realm to His kingdom, never to return alive."

Feeling was beginning to return to Garford and he surreptitiously tried flexing his fingers. They responded sluggishly but hopefully this dreadful paralysis was wearing off. It was obvious that Carrion was insane and extremely dangerous. As long as he kept on talking there was a chance that Garford could make a break for the door. If the sergeant was still alive they could possibly overcome the madman.

"You should be able to talk now, inspector. Go on, try a few words," Carrion commanded.

Garford licked his dry lips and managed to say: "How can you possibly expect me to believe all this?"

"Well, in a few moments I think you will find it very easy to believe. We're currently shifting into my Master's world and I'm afraid that your only return home will be when you die."

"I don't understand," Garford said.

Carrion drained the last drop from the glass. "Fielding and all the others have been here for the last twenty-three years. Most of them have long forgotten they were ever anywhere else in fact. They work for my Master and all they know is work, pain and death. As they passed through, they split and a perfect copy; a *simulacrum*, was left in their place. It keeps the balance right and coincidentally avoided police interference or anyone looking for missing persons, or it has done until now. The copies have no idea that they are not, strictly speaking, human and simply continue to live as the original would have done, with no knowledge of their 'twin's' plight." He grinned at Garford. "Unless you're properly insulated on the journey, the split is unavoidable." He raised his glass. "This is not whisky, it's something infinitely more precious. It allows me to stay whole. You really should have accepted a drink. The only difficulty I have in this whole setup is that when the original half of the person dies, the other follows shortly after. When that happens, the body leaves here and returns to Earth. I usually manage to clear up before anyone becomes aware but I admit I've missed a few over the years. Fielding was a nuisance, he tried to cause trouble over here and was executed in a rather *messy* if imaginative way, which resulted in lots of bits to recover. I never found the final limb." He set the glass down and reached into a pocket. From it he drew out what looked like a cigarette lighter. "I only need one more shipment of souls to receive all the power I've been promised." He took Garford's hand, forcing the palm open. "You're not my usual choice—far too old. Your sergeant will be much better, but I think I can find a use for you." He flicked open the lighter to reveal a glowing metal plate with the familiar labyrinth on it.

Garford struggled weakly but he could not prevent Carrion from pressing the red-hot metal onto his flesh. The pain was intense and the smell of his own burning flesh sickened him.

Carrion inspected the brand briefly, then moved to the sergeant.

Garford took advantage of Carrion's shift in attention. He hauled himself up from the chair, feeling his the ache in his muscles. He managed a few steps before his legs gave way and he fell to the floor.

Carrion turned at the sound. "It really is pointless. Look around you." He gestured at the room. The magnolia painted living room had faded completely, to be replaced by a cavernous room of dark stone. "We've travelled into the labyrinth."

The sickening realisation that this was truly happening flooded over Garford. It was useless to convince himself otherwise. The pattern, the labyrinth, Carrion had walked must have been his means of transporting them, abducting them—taking them from one dimension to another. How many others had he tricked into slavery over the years?

A venomous rage begin to rise in Garford's heart. Carrion was worse than any murderer he had ever encountered. Even if there was no way out for them, he could do his best to stop him from doing this again. Carrion's glass was still on the side table that now looked so incongruous. Garford grabbed it and, using all his strength, he hurled himself at the other, smashing the glass into the side of his face. To his satisfaction, Carrion let out a yell of rage and pain. Blood dripped down his hand as Garford still held the heavy base of the glass and slashed wildly for Carrion's neck, hoping to sever an artery.

Carrion leaped back out of reach and aimed a kick that sent Garford sprawling to the floor. Blood was pouring from his face where the glass had sliced into his cheek and he was panting heavily. "I see there's a violent streak in you, inspector. Excellent. I think I'll see to it that you're sent to the arena. You may even survive a fight or two." He wiped some of the blood away with his sleeve. "The simulacra of you and your sergeant will of course go back to the station. I can make them believe that there was no one at home, that John Carrion has left town." Viciously, he dragged Garford over to where his sergeant was still slumped on the floor, seemingly unconscious. "I've spent most of my life on this and there's no way that you or anyone else is going to stop me. They'll come for you soon. I'd advise you to cooperate but I doubt you'll last long either way." He opened a door Garford had not seen and was about to leave.

"Do you really think your Master will give you the power you desire?" Garford croaked desperately. While Carrion was still with them he thought there might be a chance to get home, however slim. "How do you know that he will not simply take your soul as well?"

Carrion turned in the doorway, a cold, cruel smile on his face. "Because I have faith," he replied, "and because I've already received part of my reward."

He closed his eyes for a moment and Garford watched in horror as he began to change. His hair writhed and burst into flames and when he opened his eyes, they blazed too. Garford shrank back from the sight and Carrion's terrible laughter rang in his ears as he walked away.

* * * *

The oblivious simulacra of Garford and Sergeant Hatton returned to the station. It was a disappointment that Carrion had already moved on but hopefully they might get another lead soon. Otherwise this entire investigation would have to join the list of unsolved crimes and that always irked him. Heading down to the basement, Garford found Miller and Latham absent. There were three labyrinth thumbprints on the desk; Fielding's, Cooper's and that taken from the burglar in Scotland. He still had no idea what it all meant. There were footsteps on the stairs and Miller came bursting into the room.

"Christ, Henry! Am I pleased to see you! They've found another body, headless this time but still with that damned labyrinth. Sergeant Grant radioed through ten minutes ago. He was convinced it was you at first." Miller stared at him.

"Are…you feeling all right? You don't look…"

Garford slowly raised his hand to his neck, his fingers damp from where a thin line of blood was beginning to seep out around his throat. Puzzled, he looked at his hand, noticing in the last few seconds of his life the curious mark on his thumb. A moment later, he pitched forward, his severed head rolling towards the horror-struck Miller.

CURSE OF THE DEAD

**There are some places so evil that even
the dead daren't venture inside.**

Martin Tomlin tried desperately to break through the fuzziness
and uncertainty; the mind-searing insanity which threatened to tear
him apart. He was almost ready to concede that all that he had seen
and all that he had fled from, all the blood-drenched horror, the chaos
and the supernatural powers which had been attributed to the natives,
had been real. Yet still, his brain revolted against the idea. *No!* It was
preposterous. There had to be some other, rational explanation. *There
had to be!*

Confusedly, he found himself wondering at the reality of it all…
wondering just what had happened to Harris and the interpreter, Devereaux. *Had he shot them? Had they been alive at the time?*

Some of that reality struck home as he saw the dried blood spattered all over his ripped shirt and torn trousers, his right hand shaking
where it still tensely clutched the revolver in a white-knuckled grip.

Sweat streaked his tanned, rugged face as he looked up, his mind
still reeling after the horrifying experiences of the past few hours.
Absently, he took in his immediate surroundings, seemingly for the
first time. He was sat on his haunches in the shadow of a single-story
whitewashed building, similar in many ways to those in the crude
shanties he had first visited when he had arrived in an unknown, godforsaken town in the Adamawa Region of Cameroon. It was a ram-
shackle outbuilding annexed to a long-abandoned and dusty airstrip,
its perimeter secured by a long length of head-height chain fence.
Some twenty yards away lay a pile of rusting oil drums.

Beyond the fence, for perhaps three or four miles in every direction, stretched an expanse of badland, cracked and baked by the
blazing West African sun which beat down remorselessly, soaking up
every drop of moisture from the broken land before it became the

savannah. In the far distance, beyond this hell of sun-bleached, scattered animal skeletons and the occasional stunted tree, low flat hills shimmered on the horizon.

There was no one to be seen.

Suddenly Tomlin noticed movement over to his left by the edge of the fence. Shielding his eyes against the glare, he saw a wild dog, scrawny and scarred, scrabbling in the dirt. Opening the chamber of his revolver he saw he had two bullets left.

His survival instincts had got him here, away from the immediate source of the madness and danger. However, it now seemed as though what mental and physical reserves he had remaining were yelling at him to get a grip on himself, to in some way accept what had happened and deal with it. For only by coming to terms with all that he had experienced would he be able to garner the strength of will to leave here alive. The horror had drained him of energy, paralysed him almost with dread. He was now on a precipice; faced with two decisions. To live or die.

However, having witnessed the manner of his colleagues' deaths, he got stiffly to his feet. He had come this far, but he had to go further. Despite the pain and the weariness, he had to keep moving, to put as great a distance as possible between himself and the evil that dwelled back at the village where the people still believed in the old gods, the old ways and legends; the superstitions and the ritual dances, the death-drums and the curses.

How many had there been? Twenty? Fifty? It had seemed as though the entire village had suddenly surrounded them, lurching out from the shadowed openings of their reed huts and hovels; men, women and children. Shambling, reeking, moaning figures, buzzing with flies, dressed in rags, white-eyed and drooling mouths, more corpse-like than living beings, arms outstretched, machetes and sticks in the hands of some. Devereaux had shouted a warning, and then Harris was firing, screaming, rapidly reloading, his bullets having little effect; scabrous, leathered hands grabbing him from behind, pulling him down to the sandy ground whereupon they began to brutally tear and hack him apart. Out of the corner of his eye, he had seen Devereaux struggling wildly to break free, an infant, crawling with maggots, gnawing at his shin; clawed hands bloodily tearing the flesh from his face.

Fiercely, Tomlin shook the dreadful, grisly images from his mind, aware that in their last moments his friends had been yelling at him to shoot them. He had fired and then he had turned and fled, somehow managing to break free from the ranks of foul-smelling zombies. It had been a nightmarish flight, his heart pounding as though trying to burst free, threatening to explode in his chest. He had dared not look back, fearing at any moment the rake of ragged nails across his back. Upon reaching the parked jeep he had seen that it had been wrecked; its windows smashed, its tyres slashed to ribbons.

His geographical knowledge of this area was virtually non-existent. By the position of the sun, he was able to ascertain the compass directions but having no idea where the nearest source of civilisation lay and without any means of transportation other than his feet, he knew that things were dire indeed. He gave the water canteen which hung from a strap around his shoulder a shake, gauging its contents. It was half-full, enough to perhaps last him two days at most.

The breath was rasping in his lungs as he made his way around the edge of the crude building, his finger tight around the trigger of the gun. Looking back in the direction from which he had fled, he could see where the barren ground inclined slightly, extending for perhaps a mile before reaching the sparsely-covered tree-lined escarpment.

Somewhere beyond that ridge lay the village in which the dead walked.

What madness had taken them out there? Harris had talked of diamond mines and of a long-lost temple half-buried in the earth, stuffed with age-old relics which would provide them with wealth beyond their wildest imaginings. Now he was dead, along with their French interpreter, brutally slain at the hands of things that had no right to be.

His heart lurched as a barely visible dark stick-man shape with frizzy hair appeared on the horizon. He gulped. There appeared another. And another...

For thirty terror-filled seconds he was incapable of movement as more and more scarecrow figures seemed to rise from the ground as they came over the brow of the hill; emerging like the deceased from their graves, slowly creeping like some kind of dark pestilence over the distant slope. Their movements were jerky, laboured, some stumbling before getting to their feet once more and yet there was a terrifying singleness of purpose behind their blood-fuelled advancement—to find him and to kill him, butcher him as they had his associates.

This was a bad dream. It had to be. He rubbed his eyes, raw red and stinging from the sun and the windblown grit. The shapes on the horizon were still there, swelling in numbers, getting nearer.

And then he was running, holstering his gun. At the far end of the airstrip there was an opening in the fence. Despite the fact that his legs were killing him and pain jarred through every ounce of his being, he knew that he had to keep going, that the advancing, indefatigable monstrosities, slow as they were, would be relentless in their pursuit. Even from this distance he thought he could hear their terrible wails carried on the hot, dry wind which sent the dust scurrying in mini-whirlwinds all around him. A noisome stench of death and decay struck his nostrils. It was the stink of festering carrion left to putrefy under the blistering sun.

Before him lay a long and dusty road which wound its way to the left, not quite back in the direction from which he had recently fled. There were no tyre marks visible, leading him to the assumption that this road had not been used for a very long time. He hesitated, scanning all around, weighing up his options. The terrain off-road was harsh with no visible tracks or trails which might permit easier transit across its rugged surface. It looked the kind of place where it would be all too easy to slip, to twist an ankle or break a leg. Such a mishap would surely spell disaster and for a fleeting moment he had an image of himself lying there, able only to crawl as the bloodthirsty crowd moved in. Under such circumstances there would be nothing for it but to ram the revolver into his mouth and blow his brains out.

Given the circumstances therefore he chose to take the road. Kicking up dust with every step, he began to jog, maintaining a pace which, admittedly not breakneck, was still increasing the distance between himself and his pursuers. To go any faster would achieve little but exhaust him quicker, requiring him to pause and rest—a luxury which he could not afford. His sweat-soaked shirt now stuck uncomfortably to his back.

He had been going for close on ten minutes when, with some dismay, he noticed that the track he was following headed back towards the jungle. He was faced with a decision—either continue in the hope that the road skirted the village or, if he was lucky, and fast, backtrack and head off into the wilderness. How long he could keep going he had no idea…an hour? Two hours? He was tired and thirsty, suffering from shock after having faced something that no one should ever have to witness. It seemed as though fire was burning through his limbs and his nerves were tingling. Something had obviously struck him as he had fought his way free of the undead mob for there was a dull, throbbing pain in his right shoulder.

The jungle was wide and stretched for mile after mile in every direction. It would offer some shelter from the boiling heat which soaked down into every portion of his body, loosening his muscles like flowing wax and yet it harboured its own dangers—a place where death could strike suddenly and swiftly. However, it could also provide cover. Perhaps within its dark interior he could not only outdistance them, but throw them completely off his scent.

Wiping the sweat from his face, Tomlin stopped, shoulders hunched, eyes alert, focusing on the greenness that lay ahead. Not all of it was as dense as he had first anticipated. Through the trees before him, he saw that the jungle thinned out appreciably a couple of hundred yards in front and there was a grassy hillock, sloping down to the muddy waters of a sluggish river, fringed with tall reeds and broad-leafed plants. Thick clouds of large insects buzzed and hovered over its brown-blue, murky surface. Vines and creepers trailed from the many thin-trunked trees. Long neglected, the track had become fairly overgrown and yet he still figured that it provided him with the best means of escape.

Looking behind him, due to the lie of the land, he could see none of his ghastly pursuers. Yet, he knew they were still out there, edging their way after him, perhaps a mile or more behind. There was an uncanniness in the manner in which they knew exactly where he was going; a dark intelligence which guided them, instructed them. It was as though their actions were being controlled by some dammed power which knew instinctively what he was doing and where he was going.

A subtle change in the direction of the wind brought with it that putrid stink which confirmed his belief.

Heart thumping, Tomlin entered the jungle. Inside, the sunlight was dappled, filtering through the trees and vegetation, throwing weird shadows across his path. He could now see that the trail led around one side of the hillock, skirting the river before heading back into the jungle interior. Jogging along, his heart sank to find that in some places, nearer the river, the road had become marshy, impeding his progress. Why anyone would construct what he assumed had once been a functional road out here was beyond him. Sometime in the past it had obviously been connected to the airstrip. As to where it led…

There was a dull thumping in his head. Blood was coursing through his temples. Whether it was down to fear, exhaustion or the heat and the pain, his vision swam, the images before him wavering as his legs buckled. Reaching out for a slender tree trunk, he managed to support himself. For a moment his mind blanked, darkened, and this time he did lose his footing, crumpling to the ground.

He could not have been out for long, a minute, probably less, when he pulled himself to his feet, suffering from mild disorientation.

Unsteadily, he began walking, picking up his pace a little. There was now movement all around; small shapes leaping in the canopy overhead, rustling in the undergrowth. Oinking loudly, something that looked like a cross between a large rat and a small pig scurried across his path barely ten feet in front of him, its sudden movements startling him, making him reach for his gun.

Like a dead man himself, Tomlin stumbled and staggered along the track, deeper into the jungle, now largely oblivious to the plethora of strange, shrill animal calls all around. The dry, searing heat of the open plains had now given way to an uncomfortable humidity. His shirt was sodden with perspiration. After the best part of an hour, he began to lose all track of time and distance as the going became increasingly harder. In his mind's eye, he could envisage those loathsome beings shambling and crawling after him, guided in his direction by an unholy power.

Soon, he would be unable to continue. He would have to stop and rest, the exhaustion he now felt throughout his body, crippling. Up ahead, this patch of jungle thinned out once more. Was that a road in front of him?

And then he heard it. The sound of a mechanised vehicle of some sort.

Desperately, Tomlin urged his aching body to make the effort. Arms raised, he rushed forward, frantically hoping that he could flag down the driver. He was still some thirty yards from the junction when the rusty, ancient-looking, slow-moving agricultural vehicle went past, its white-skinned operator perched high at a huge steering wheel. Bearing a strong resemblance to a survivor from some natural disaster or a refugee from a war-torn settlement, Tomlin half-fell, emerging from the undergrowth onto the earthen road. "*Help! Stop!*" he yelled, hoarsely.

The huge machine, half-tractor, half-combine harvester, showed no signs of slowing.

There was nothing else for it. Tomlin drew out his gun and fired a shot into the air, the loud report sending a flock of large-winged birds skyward from their perches.

This time the vehicle stopped, the driver throwing a curious backward glance.

Staggering forwards, Tomlin waved his arms, hoping that the other would recognise and understand his actions, realise that, despite the fact that he had a loaded gun, he posed no threat. "Wait. Please wait!"

Warily, the man shouted something back in French, something that Tomlin failed to understand. Still, he had made no move to speed off.

Aware that he still had his revolver in his hand, Tomlin returned it to his holster, hoping that this action would demonstrate an unthreatening stance. He was now less than ten feet away, close enough to see that the driver was exceptionally ugly. There was an overall unpleasantness about the man's features which were mercifully shaded by the wide-brimmed hat he wore. Something about his general appearance; the slightly bulging eyes and the wide mouth gave him a rather toadish look. Even his bare arms which protruded from his dirty jerkin, were mottled and unhealthy looking whether due to some kind of tropical disease or over-exposure to the sun.

Tomlin did not have much time to give the other his full appraisal however. For, now that he had returned his gun to his holster, the driver suddenly pulled a shotgun on him.

A stream of watery-sounding French words spewed threateningly out of the man's mouth.

"Don't shoot! For the love of God, don't shoot!" With a nervous gulp, Tomlin raised his hands once more.

A cruel-looking sneer spread over the other's thick, rubbery lips. His shotgun trained on Tomlin, he motioned for him to get on board.

* * * *

Ten minutes later, the road they were taking veered around the edge of a large plantation. Tomlin could see figures working in the fields, although his mind was more concerned with the shotgun still levelled at him, held, admittedly unsteadily, in the hand of the driver. It had been a bumpy ride, the large farmyard vehicle churning up and ejecting huge clods of earth and mud in its wake. Throughout the journey, the driver had said nothing, adding to the overall feeling of menace.

There had been the occasional moment when Tomlin thought he might have been able to overpower the other, to take him off-balance but he had decided, perhaps wisely, that such action was not without its own risks. A pull of the trigger and it could all be over. Perhaps once they arrived at wherever they were going he might be fortunate enough to find someone who spoke English, someone to whom he could explain his predicament.

Whether or not he would be believed was another question.

Regardless of the precariousness of his current situation, he felt some relief at the knowledge that he was getting further and further away from the zombie threat. Surely now there was little or no chance of them being able to catch up with him.

The road widened somewhat and he could now see that they were approaching a large, yet somewhat decaying, house built in the French colonial style similar in many ways to buildings he had once seen in Louisiana. Two storied, its pillared entrance was broad, flanked on either sides by tall trees, intertwined with creepers. Many of the windows were shuttered, the paintwork faded and peeling. The roof had sagged in places and despite its once grandiose architectural design it now bore signs of great decrepitude. There was something unsettling about it, an eeriness that disturbed Tomlin. He tried not to imagine what the place would look like when it got dark.

Muttering a curse, the odd driver brought the farmyard vehicle to a stop. Despite his bulk, he jumped down agilely and motioned for Tomlin to do likewise. He then stepped back, his shotgun trained on his passenger's every move, gesturing for him to make for the run-down mansion.

Tomlin knew he had one bullet remaining. In his mind he was toying with the idea of seeing whether or not he could take the other by surprise, wondering whether he might be able to avoid getting shot, that was of course assuming that the other's shotgun was loaded. Then, if he was lucky, he might be able to get in a killing hit. It would then just be a case of seeing whether or not he could start up the tractor or whatever it was and see about getting the hell out of here. It was whilst he was considering his options, that, out of the corner of his eye, he saw the front door of the mansion open.

Coming along the drive was a slim, smartly-dressed, bespectacled man who appeared to be in his early fifties. He cried out something in French and the toad-faced individual slouched back towards his vehicle.

"I need help." Tomlin looked somewhat relieved. It appeared that someone normal was now on the scene.

"Monsieur," said the bespectacled man. "You are English, yes?" It was abundantly clear that he was French.

Tomlin nodded. "Yes. You're not going to believe what's happened. I badly need your assistance."

"Yes, I can see that." Critically, the other looked Tomlin up and down. "But first let's get inside the house." He turned and began to march briskly to the front door, Tomlin limping somewhat behind him.

* * * *

"Zombies?" The owner of the mansion, who had introduced himself as Raymond Saint-Yves, poured two glasses of brandy and handed one over to Tomlin.

Tomlin accepted the proffered glass. "I'm telling you what I saw. They murdered my two companions before my very eyes." He took a sip. There was something about his host that struck him as just not right, something indefinable, yet definitely there. He had now been in the mansion for fifteen minutes or so, during which time he had been given the opportunity to wash much of the grime and the blood from his body and to slake his thirst. Unfortunately, his host had no spare clothes in his size so he was still in his torn and dusty shirt and trousers. Of greater concern, however, was the fact that there was no phone, no means of communication with the outside world. He was still worried, concerned that those undead villagers may still be after him. If such were the case and if they had the means of tracking him, then it would surely only be a matter of time before they turned up here.

"Then perhaps the old legends of the *vekongi* are true," mused Saint-Yves, casually. They were in a cool and shadowy room, its windows shuttered. Several items of Central and West African exotica; native hide shields, spears, zebra hides and lion heads adorned the walls. "It's been long-rumoured among some of the lesser well-known offshoots of the *Bakweri* that the *vekongi*—the zombies that you speak of—are created by *nyongo*-priests, similar in many ways to the *bokors* who practice voodoo."

"I don't know anything about that and to be honest, that should be the least of our concerns. I take it that you have guns here? If you take my advice, you should round up as many men as you have and post guards. I'm telling you, that entire village that we had the misfortune of entering was filled with them." Tomlin drained his glass and put it on a desk. He knew it would do no good to just sit here, waiting to see if those horrors turned up. Perhaps even now they were entering the plantations he had passed earlier. In which case very soon there would be a mad rush of farmyard labourers hammering at the doors. "We can't just sit here and wait on their arrival."

"What would you suggest that I do?" Saint-Yves spoke quietly and calmly. Either he did not believe a single word that Tomlin was saying or he was not in the least worried about the prospect of a small army of mindless, unstoppable killers, undoubtedly eager for human flesh, turning up on his doorstep.

"Look, mister, you've got to believe me!" Tomlin's tone was surly. "There are things out there that murdered two of my friends. I'm not sure whether guns are any good against them." Upon noticing his host's blatantly unconcerned look, he launched himself forward, grabbing the other by the lapels of his smart jacket. "*Are you listening to me?* Do you understand what I'm saying?" He looked intently into the man's eyes.

Saint-Yves was startled, shaken.

Breathing heavily, Tomlin released his hold. "Maybe you don't understand."

Warily, Saint-Yves backed away. It was clear that he was not used to being so roughly handled. "You're beginning to scare me, monsieur. All of this talk of zombies making their way through the jungle. Please try and see it from my position. Surely you have to appreciate it is all a little hard to accept?"

"It's the truth. I'm telling you." Tomlin's pounding headache was coming back. Despite the coolness, he felt a rivulet of sweat dribble down his face and there was an unwelcome prickling sensation at the back of his throat. He staggered to one side as his vision suddenly blurred. It appeared as though there were now three spinning images of Saint-Yves before him. His brain was swimming, reeling. Fiercely, he tried to get a grip on himself yet his legs now felt like jelly. For a moment or two he was certain that he was going to die right there and then, certain that the other had poisoned him. With that terrible thought rushing through his swirling brain he made two lumbering steps forward, arms extended, before collapsing to the floor.

* * * *

Tomlin came out of one nightmare straight into another, a waking one this time. Upon opening his eyes he found himself lying on the floor of a cage-like trailer attached to a vehicle, a dozen or so of his fellow 'passengers' strewn around him. All of them were undoubtedly dead; withered, leathery beings. Two or three of them bore ghastly wounds and one of them was blackened and blistered as though it had been terribly burnt. It was only with a great effort of will that he stopped himself from screaming out loud for he was in the midst of this gruesome corpse-pile; an arm which had been partially worm-eaten was draped over his chest and a badly decayed head was slumped against his shoulder. Flies swarmed everywhere and the stink was terrible.

A sickening horror crashed down on him. Madness threatened to consume him. Savagely, he shook off the weight of dark-skinned dead flesh under which he had been lying and got himself to his feet, aware that his captors had taken his gun. Now that he could see things better, he felt like retching. Nausea swelled from the pit of his stomach into his throat as he thrust both of his hands against the bars, gripping them, shaking. He was convulsing, as yet unaware of the nascent daylight just beginning to wash the broken landscape in the first golden rays of the day.

His chest was heaving as he slowly began to take laboured breaths, filling his lungs. The trailer was being towed by that strange agricultural vehicle he had seen previously. Seated at the wheel, their backs to him, were two men—the hatted, toad-faced freak and Saint-Yves.

Tomlin spat to clear his throat. "You bastards! Where are you taking me?" he yelled.

Saint-Yves turned in his seat and gave a little wave. He then said something to the driver who emitted a gargling laugh.

"I'll kill you both when I get out of here!" Tomlin raved. Feebly, he tried to break the bars but it was no good. Unsteadily, largely due to the prone bodies on the floor and the bouncing of the vehicle, he crossed over to the gate at the rear of the cage-covered trailer. It had been locked and bolted. He shook it nonetheless. "Let me out, damn you!"

The vehicle continued to lurch from side to side.

Not wanting to look down at the stinking bodies which shared the trailer with him and fully aware that his cries for release were getting him nowhere, Tomlin turned his gaze on his surroundings. Now that dawn had broken he could see that they were following a dusty track which seemed to be out in the middle of nowhere—a truly godforsaken, deserted, barren plain which stretched in all directions to the distant, flat horizons. For all he knew they had been travelling all night and were now many miles away from where they had set out. As they progressed, on either side of the track, he saw curiously humped, sand-covered mounds. Behind them, visible even through the dust and grit kicked up by the tyres, a sand storm had blown up and he could make it out quite clearly as it scudded over the rocky desert, the sand whirled high by the wind, lifting it into the brightening heavens like an army of infernal devils off to do battle.

How much longer would the torment go on for? Tomlin's mind was working overtime going through a hundred dark scenarios; trying to guess just why he was being brought out here. It seemed an inordinate length to go to just to murder him, after all there were countless closer places where his body could be dumped if that was the reason behind all of this. Then again, he had heard of an illegal slave trade still flourishing in this part of Africa. Maybe Saint-Yves was involved in such nefarious activity and was now taking him to some terrible unknown slum where he would be forced into shackles and paraded before the wicked slavers; auctioned like cattle—sold into a life of painful servitude to the highest bidder.

Then, through the bars of his cage, Tomlin saw it.

Rising from the sand and the rubble, its stone walls covered in places by great zigzagging cracks, was an ancient domed edifice. Wooden scaffolding had been erected up one wall and he could see figures milling around like ants, clearing away the veritable mountain of windblown sand which had encroached it, burying it almost. The air was filled with choking dust. The whole scene reminded him of the several archaeological excavations he had seen in Mesopotamia and Egypt. And then it struck him. *This had to be the temple Harris had mentioned!*

They came to a bone-jarring halt.

Tomlin stared at his captors as they came round to the trailer. The ugly man with the hat held his shotgun.

"Well, I do hope you enjoyed the ride," said Saint-Yves. "You know it really was most unfortunate that you and your friends entered Mzolo. It's the only village in which the *vekongi* are kept in a constant state of activity in the need to keep interlopers, such as yourself, away."

Tomlin said nothing, his eyes boring into the other, willing him dead.

"Regardless, you now have two choices, monsieur. Either you cooperate…or you die. The choice is yours." Saint-Yves swatted away a large black fly that had alighted on his sleeve. "Let me offer you a proposition."

"Burn in Hell!" Tomlin spat.

Saint-Yves smiled. "And here I am trying to be reasonable." He sighed and muttered something to the toad-faced man before facing Tomlin once more. "Monsieur, my friend here can make life very unpleasant for you. And I mean *very* unpleasant."

"If you're going to shoot me then shoot me and get it over with," snarled Tomlin, defiantly.

Saint-Yves' smile widened and he emitted a little private laugh. He shook his head slightly. "Something far worse than that, I'm afraid." He gestured to his accomplice. "Perhaps a little demonstration is needed."

'Toad-Face' passed Saint-Yves the shotgun. With a flabby hand, he brought out a black stone pendant which hung around his deeply-lined neck and began to chant.

Tomlin gulped, not knowing what to expect.

Accompanied by an obscene moaning, life returned to the dead at his feet!

With jerky movements they began to twitch and quiver, their actions more puppet-like than that of a normal human being.

Tomlin's eyes nearly popped out of his head as he stared at the dreadful spectacle before him. He was certain that once they arose fully and sensed his *differentness* the mindless horrors would set upon him; tear him to pieces as they had his friends. Given the circumstances, getting shot was one thing he was quite prepared to accept but to be savagely dismembered and devoured... "*Make it stop!* I'll do whatever you say!" he yelled.

"Are you sure?" Saint-Yves asked.

"For God's sake... *Yes!*" Wildly, Tomlin was shaking the bars, glancing over his shoulder as the zombies began to stir.

"*Absolutely* sure?" Saint-Yves was dragging this out, relishing in the fear and the power he had over his captive. He was grinning cruelly, delighting in this torment.

"*Get me out!*" Tomlin was screaming now, frantically shaking the cage, bordering on the hysterical.

With a brief nod to 'Toad-Face', Saint-Yves acknowledged the hold he had on his prisoner. Instantly, the chanting ceased. The ugly man with the hat shouted out something else in a bizarre language and waved his pendant. The dead flopped to the floor of the trailer, lifeless and unmoving once more.

"Now that I believe we have reached some kind of understanding, I will let you into a little secret," said Saint-Yves. "Many years ago my father came out to Africa when this part of the world was still a French colony. He was a brilliant archaeologist who became dissatisfied with the purely academic side of the discipline, openly refuting the many scholarly claims regarding the advent of African civilisation, challenging the orthodox chronologies. He was not interested in studying the settlement patterns of the Early Sao or the Late Urewe cultures that dotted this landscape. From his reading, he became convinced that an inhuman species who worshipped Demogorgon reigned supreme in this area long before man had mastered the working of iron, animal husbandry or the building of any kind of permanent structure. Right up until his death, he remained adamant that somewhere in this region there existed a temple, built not by men, but by this ancient race." He waved an arm, gesturing to the half-revealed edifice. "This is what you can see. Unfortunately, my father died before it was discovered. Count yourself lucky for you are only the third living person to ever see this place. As you have no doubt figured out, I use the *vekongi* for all of the manual work; the digging and the clearing, in addition to working on my plantation. They're an extremely effective workforce. They never tire. They follow orders without hesitation. They don't complain or argue with my decisions and they don't need water or food. Nor do they need paying, which is probably for the best considering the work is a never-ending process. We are continuously having to ensure that the one entrance so far discovered remains clear of windblown sand. I've ordered them to keep digging in the hope that there are other entrances which will no doubt lead to even deeper levels."

"Why have you brought me here?" asked Tomlin wearily.

"A good question." There was a wicked glint in Saint-Yves' eyes. He smiled briefly before replying. "Well, you see this is where the *vekongi's* sole weakness lies. For, despite their usefulness it appears that they're unable to enter the temple—if indeed it is a temple. Some power or other prevents them from setting foot inside. It could be that a latent fear or a deep-rooted superstition remains within them. Nevertheless, this is a problem which you alone can solve."

"You want me to go in there? Why don't you go in?"

"I've been in."

Tomlin did not like the sounds of any of this but he disliked even more the prospect of remaining caged alongside these horrors just waiting for them to stir. "Are there traps?" he asked, well aware that many of the old tombs he had explored over the course of his chequered past had been riddled with cunning devices primed to kill or trap the unwary.

Saint-Yves didn't answer. He reached into a jacket pocket, removed a key and unlocked the trailer-gate.

'Toad-Face' gestured with his shotgun for Tomlin to get out.

* * * *

The excavation was enormous. It was only as Tomlin got closer, 'Toad-Face' walking just behind him and Saint-Yves in front, that he began to truly appreciate the immense scale of the clearance project, all of which had been done without recourse to mechanised heavy lifting equipment for there were no cranes or bulldozers. Mountains of sand, rock and earth had been quarried away by picks and shovels; cleared away by the tireless zombie workforce and whereas other such sites would possibly have resonated with the chanting of work-songs, here there was nothing of the sort, just the ceaseless grating of metal on stone and the savage gusting of the wind.

Tomlin guessed there must have been at least two hundred of them; their bodies dust and sand-covered; undead slaves doomed to work in this truly hellish place. The Frenchman and his ugly sidekick must have been rounding up the inhabitants of the neighbouring villages, converting the living into these dreadful abominations by the use of the *nyongo* black magic. If they hadn't been dead, he could almost have felt some remorse for their plight.

Overhead, the sky had now turned a sickly shade of tangerine, lending the place a weird, unearthly, almost Martian atmosphere. Great clouds of dust and grit billowed and eddied, scouring exposed flesh and making the eyes sting. The *vekongi* continued in their work, oblivious to the harsh conditions.

After having passed through a long avenue lined with high columns upon whose time-eroded surfaces faint, obscene pictograms were vaguely visible, Saint-Yves came to a stop. He turned and waited for Tomlin to draw up alongside. "Amazing, I'm sure you'd agree." He had to raise his voice to be heard in the grit-swirling blizzard. "It has remained undiscovered for over a hundred thousand years and has no known name. There are references to it, of course, in some of the ancient works and in the oral traditions handed down among the more obscure and degenerative ancestors of the Bakweri."

A winding wooden walkway formed from stout planks enabled access up the vast mound of sand before them. A lifeless wretch, pushing a heavily-laden wheelbarrow was descending the ramp. Saint-Yves waited for it to reach the bottom whereupon it shambled to one side in order to dispose of its pile of rubble.

Despite the fear and loathing that was coursing through his veins, Tomlin found himself staring about, wide-eyed, awestruck by the sheer fantasticalness of it all. It was like something out of a terrible dream. Surely this was something that man was never meant to see. Something that should have remained forever buried. It reeked of blasphemy and corruption and there was an almost tangible wickedness about it; a pervasive aura of aeon-long evil which seemed to have leached into the very fabric of the building. The walls were formed of massive, cyclopean stonework; faint traces of indiscernible murals barely visible, the artistry unlike anything he had ever seen before.

"At the top of the ramp is the entrance," said Saint-Yves. "Follow me."

Despairingly, Tomlin knew that escape was impossible. He might possibly be able to swiftly turn around, take 'Toad-Face' by surprise, overpower him and snatch the shotgun but it would then be only a matter of seconds before he found himself encircled by ranks of zombies. And yet, he didn't like the thought of having to venture inside this half-buried, unhallowed cathedral or whatever it was supposed to have once been

"No tricks, monsieur," warned Saint-Yves as though he had read Tomlin's thoughts. "My friend *will* shoot you, but he will not kill you. That task will be left to my workers."

On leaden feet, Tomlin was herded up the wooden ramp. He tried to rid his mind of the dreadful feeling that he was climbing to his doom—and that, like a sacrificial victim, he would meet some grisly end once he reached the top. Despite their sturdiness, the planks creaked with each step.

Saint-Yves raised a hand and came to a stop. "This is it." He gestured to a dark opening in the outer wall. A thick length of rope, which had been tightly secured to a large rock, snaked inside. "Unfortunately it's a drop of about twenty feet to the ground level, hence the rope."

Tomlin edged closer. He now knew that to venture inside was suicide. He would never come out again. Saint-Yves would make sure of that—pulling up the rope as soon as he was down there. With that thought coursing through his mind, and knowing that he was a dead man whatever happened, he made a sudden, desperate lunge at the Frenchman, not caring whether his actions would result in him getting shot and fed to the ghastly labourers or not. Grabbing him savagely around the throat, he swung him around, effectively using him as a human shield should 'Toad-Face' decide to shoot.

Struggling, the Frenchman tried to break the hold but Tomlin only tightened his grip, dragging the other to one side. And then 'Toad-Face' was bounding towards them, clearly not knowing whether to risk a shot or not.

Still gripping Saint-Yves around the neck, Tomlin smacked in two solid kidney punches, spinning his foe around. Then, with a gargling cry, 'Toad-Face' now within striking distance himself, launched a vicious kick which caught Tomlin on the left shin, making him cry out in pain. Still, he maintained his grip.

And then all three of them crashed together, slipping on the wooden planking in a riot of curses.

Punching and kicking, scrabbling insanely, Tomlin's main concern was to get the shotgun. He had always been a dirty fighter, having been in enough brawls over the years to know that chivalry went by the wayside when one was fighting for survival. Lunging out, his right foot connected painfully with 'Toad-Face's' groin. Grabbing a handful of sand, Tomlin swept it up, throwing it directly into the other's eyes. A powerful right hook sent Saint-Yves reeling. He then struggled to his feet, eyes searching frantically for the dropped shotgun. Upon noticing it, he crouched down and was just about to snatch it up when, uttering a gargling cry, 'Toad-Face' came rushing forward.

Tomlin met the onward charge. He grappled with the other, spinning him around and hurling him forward.

With a scream, the unfortunate landed, head-first, on the rock around which the rope was fastened.

Tomlin winced at the bone-jarring crack, watching as the other rolled on to his back, blood streaming from his flattened nose and his mashed lips.

It took a moment for the wretch to open his jaws, both upper and lower sets of teeth having clamped and splintered together, and when he did so, it was to spit out a lump of glistening tongue. In a final act, born of desperation, 'Toad-Face' removed the black-stone pendant and, in words that came forth in a bloody drool, shouted something. He then slumped to the sand.

Looking over his shoulder, Tomlin's heart sank upon seeing the dark shapes gathering at the base of the ramp. A dozen or so of them began the awkward ascent as he lifted the shotgun. "Call them off!" he shouted to Saint-Yves who stood to one side, nursing his injuries.

The Frenchman was stunned and in obvious pain. His glasses had been broken and he stared uncertainly, his vision blurred. Half-heartedly, he shuffled over to his fallen companion.

The *vekongi* were getting nearer.

"He's out...I think he's dead," Saint-Yves whimpered. Grasping the pendant, he tore it free. "I don't have the power to use it."

"You'd better do something fast you son of a bitch," Tomlin snarled. Below him, the vast ranks of the undead were now mobilising, moving slowly, yet inexorably, towards them. No longer under the direct control of the *nyongo*-priest it appeared that they had now reverted back to their feral, disorderly state.

Saint-Yves raised the pendant. It had no effect whatsoever.

There were now trapped with but one possibility of escape. If they wanted to survive they had no option but to go where the dead would not follow...

The chamber into which Tomlin lowered himself was roughly circular in plan. He had been unable to climb down with the shotgun so he had left it outside.

Saint-Yves had gone down first and was now groping in the darkness for the bag he had left down here the last time he had ventured inside. He found it and removed a high-powered torch.

"Do you know what's down here?" Tomlin asked bitterly. "And more importantly, do you think there's another way out?" Above him, he could see several hollowed-out faces leering down. At least the zombies lacked the intelligence to pull up the rope, not that he thought they would get the chance to climb back out any time soon. In all likelihood they were entombed here forever.

The Frenchman shook his head.

"You know, I should kill you here and now," said Tomlin angrily, snatching the torch from the other's limp grasp. "However, you may prove useful if there *are* any traps." Shining the light around, he could see that they were at the sand-covered base of some sort of weird tower. An arched opening in one wall appeared to offer the only way forward. He peered into the tunnel.

"Monsieur—"

"Shut up!" Tomlin snapped. He strained his senses, fearing that he had heard something. A few terror-filled seconds flitted past. His mind was playing havoc; concocting all manner of horrible things—monsters born of nightmare, ready to emerge from the shadows. That there was evil here was undeniable. "We go this way."

The air was hot and dusty. The tunnel they entered was narrow and low-ceilinged and the further they went the more confined their surroundings became. Every so often crumbling stonework would drizzle down, giving the worrying impression that the entire structure was about to collapse about them, burying them at any moment in an avalanche of rubble and sand.

After a few minutes, the passage began to slope gently downwards and as they started down the decline, they soon noticed portions of the wall adorned with strange murals depicting bizarre rituals. Shrunken, cowled beings resembling a horrible human-serpent hybrid featured strongly, their preponderance increasing the further they traversed, until whole stretches of wall were thus covered.

There was an otherworldly atmosphere about this place—a strong sense of detachment from the normal, sane world that Tomlin had now all but forgotten. A vast vaulted chamber opened before them and by the light from the torch they could see that the floor was in actuality a great, circular stele; a massive slab over a hundred feet in diameter which had undoubtedly taken an aeon to carve for this was no mere piece of art or some elaborate pit covering.

"Christ! What *is* this?" Tomlin stared in horror-drenched fascination. He took several stumbling steps forward.

The patterns on the floor had been made with the utmost precision, each angle and curve conforming to specific, sacred, geometrical measurements. In addition, the entire face of the slab sloped, almost imperceptibly, towards the centre, where there was a circular opening. Looking down, Tomlin saw that narrow channels had been incorporated into this feature, and his heart sank upon realising that it had been designed so that it permitted the draining of some liquid or other—probably blood—from points on the circumference of the slab. This blood would then cover the surface with its crimson embrace before being funnelled into the aperture in the middle. In effect, it was a huge sacrificial disc, similar in many ways to Aztec glyphstones he had seen, only much larger.

There came an ominous *click*. Tomlin spun round. Saint-Yves stood before him, a revolver, which he must have had kept concealed on his person, pointed straight at him. There was a maniacal glint in the Frenchman's eyes.

"*Demogorgon!* Lord of the Bottomless Pit! Arise and accept this sacrifice!" Saint-Yves raised the gun.

Instinctively, Tomlin switched off the torch and leapt to one side. A gunshot rang out, followed by a second and a third. All three bullets missed their mark, ricocheting with a shrill whine off the far wall.

In the utter blackness, Tomlin moved as quietly as he could, circling the Frenchman's position, clipping the torch to his belt.

A fourth random shot shattered the darkness. Saint-Yves cursed.

And then Tomlin was behind him, strong hands around his neck, forcing him down to his knees.

Saint-Yves tried to squirm, to turn the revolver on his attacker but Tomlin reacted fast, grabbing his foe by the wrist and forcing the gun towards the Frenchman's head. Hands trembling, the two men were locked in a battle of strength as each tried to gain control of the gun.

Tomlin however was the stronger and he had a better grip and position. He was just about to bring his own finger down on the trigger, when a surprise elbow jab from Saint-Yves knocked the wind from him.

The gun fell to the ground.

And then, like a man possessed, Saint-Yves leapt at Tomlin. Snarling, he launched several punches, smacking two quick-fire jabs into Tomlin's ribs, the pain causing him to double-up.

Recovering quickly, Tomlin caught hold of one of his attacker's arms and hauled him close, his other hand reaching out and grabbing a handful of thinning hair. He pulled violently, ripping it from his assailant's scalp, before bringing the head down to meet his rising knee, the blow sending the other sprawling. He reached for the torch and switched it on. The revolver lay at his feet. In a fluid motion he gathered it up, aiming straight at Saint-Yves who now stood at the great disk's edge, blood trickling from the fingers of the hand clamped to his lower face.

For a brief moment it seemed as though time had stood still—creating a bizarre tableau; a reversal of the situation only a minute or so before.

A dark red spot of blood dripped from Saint-Yves' hand, landing on the seal.

More and more blood fell. Soon it was leaking from the Frenchman's busted nose and lips as he stared in confused horror. The leak became a gush, blood erupting in a scarlet torrent that was drawn to the channels incised within the carving on the floor.

Revolver gripped tightly, Tomlin stepped back. A rush of black insanity threatened to claim him, to drag him off to the dark places from which few, if any, ever returned. He stared as Saint-Yves began to shrivel before his very eyes as an inordinate amount of blood was literally drawn out of him. It then began to flow, directed, spiralling along the convoluted channel which encircled the central aperture, the redness forming a monstrous, leering, demonic face.

There was nothing he could do but stand and watch, spellbound with morbid curiosity.

And then the blood was vanishing, disappearing completely into the central aperture, leaving no trace of its passage, no staining whatsoever.

A disturbing silence fell. A silence pregnant with dread expectation.

An abrupt tremor shook the chamber.

Shielding his head from falling stonework, Tomlin retreated further into the passage which led back.

A series of explosions sounded from deep below. Bizarre, purplish-green fumes belched forth from the hole in the ground. With a loud crack, a huge zigzagging fissure rent the great slab and a massive, grey-green scaled tentacle emerged, its pale yellow underside covered with ugly suckers.

Saint-Yves' deflated corpse was thrown into the air like a rag doll. The Frenchman's blood-drained remains bounced off the chamber ceiling and fell to the ground with a sickening splat.

Madness screamed at Tomlin. Firing off the remaining two shots, he turned and fled as behind him, the ancient chthonic demon began to pull itself free, its actions accompanied by a hellish chorus of unearthly wailing which echoed off the crumbling, mural-covered walls. It was as though Hell itself had come to claim the Earth, its presence heralded by a choir of fallen angels.

An explosive blast of dust and detritus struck him as the chamber ceiling collapsed. Screaming, Tomlin dashed back to where he had first entered this unhallowed pit. He made for the dangling rope, and began to frantically pull himself up, not caring what might be waiting for him on the outside. There were degrees of evil, and that possessed by the nightmare he had just seen far surpassed that of the *vekongi*.

For one terrible moment he felt certain that the rope was going to give way, and that he would plummet to the ground. However, it held, and with some relief he hauled himself free.

Massed ranks of zombies were staggering and shuffling away from the mound, a heap of them lay writhing at the base, eager to escape, no doubt sensing Demogorgon's release.

Tomlin snatched up the fallen shotgun. He then ransacked 'Toad-Face's' corpse for the keys to the vehicle that had brought him to this accursed site. He was just about to start running when, with a violent upheaval, the top half of the mound, building and all, started to subside, sinking in on itself in a great implosion of rock, debris and dust. Blinded, he felt himself falling, but instead of being devoured by the mound and the nest of giant, writhing tentacles which had now burst forth, he managed to jump to one side, so that, as the whole thing collapsed, he slid and tumbled on the terrible avalanche that was formed. Crashing and screaming, a mountain of rubble, sand and wooden planking in pursuit, he continued to fall, his world darkening and flashing through his brain in one almighty, all-smothering descent.

Choking, coughing, spinning—Tomlin's nightmare seemed to go on and on until, with a bone-jarring thump, he hit the ground. It seemed impossible that he was still alive and it was only the pain in his battered body that confirmed this. All was dark. Sudden terror struck him upon realising that he was buried and that he would soon suffocate. Panic leant him strength as he began to tunnel his way free.

Luckily for him he was not that deeply buried.

Spitting dust from his mouth, Tomlin crawled out of the mass of sand and debris. Only a handful of zombies remained in the excavation site, and those were shuffling away. He threw a backward glance. The edifice had been almost completely destroyed, reduced to rubble, and as he stared three more huge tentacles erupted from within, crushing and grasping whatever they fell on, constricting and crushing walls; pulverizing them to powder. Electric-blue flashes and more muffled explosions shook the now almost flattened mound. Fissures cracked open, venting noisome gases.

Frantically, he scrambled to his feet, pain lancing through his right leg. Limping, he went as fast as he could, heading for where his abductors had parked their vehicle. He was soon rushing alongside the ranks of the terror-driven undead, pushing them aside.

The sky was darkening. It had become an unhealthy-looking shade of purple.

Chaos swept down like a plummeting vulture, striking him like a living thing. That unearthly wailing—that cacodemonical cacophony of the damned—picked up in strength. Despair seized his heart and soul in a grip as cold as death. A shadow began to fall around him.

Through the wind and the rain and the mass of festering flesh he battled his way. Yelling insanely, Tomlin reached the parked vehicle. He threw up the shotgun and clambered onboard. His hand was shaking as he fiercely turned the key in the ignition. A cloud of black exhaust fumes belched out as the machine lurched forward. And then he was throwing the gears, moving forward, turning the large steering wheel.

Uncaringly, he mowed down hordes of the departing undead, grinding their remains into the dusty track. Obscene splashes of dark grey-red blood spattered the bonnet. A severed head and arm landed in the seat next to him. They were still moving; the fingers of the hand flexing, the eyeballs and mouth of the head twitching. Pedal to the floor, he kept going, the vehicle bouncing as it trundled over the heaps of corpses. One zombie got snagged in the bars of the trailer-cage and got dragged along.

He must have gone the best part of a third of a mile…*and yet, the shadow continued to fall around him!* The sight he saw in his rear-view mirror hammered home the futility of his escape and brought insanity crashing down upon him. For the thing he saw rising from the ruins was as enormous as it was diabolical; a loathsome entity that towered high into the sky of which the writhing tentacles were but the upper most part. A great clawed hand extended and reached out for him and it was all he could do to swerve to one side, grab the shotgun and leap out as, tyres spinning, the vehicle tipped over.

The demon picked up the tractor and pulped it in its grip.

Tomlin screamed and laughed hysterically. He thrust the barrel into his mouth and pulled the trigger.

THE RESURRECTION OF NICHOLAS ZEGREMBI

Over the course of history there have been many threats to mankind—but it has yet to face its gravest challenge.

Jeremiah Mason was a tall man with sunken cheekbones which gave him a gaunt, almost cadaverous look, thinning grey hair and piercing blue eyes. An investigative parapsychologist, a leading authority on the occult and a delver into the esoteric; at sixty-six he now classed himself as semi-retired. For over forty years he had applied his encyclopaedic mind to researching and investigating numerous supernatural mysteries, applying his considerable erudition to countless bizarre cases throughout Britain.

What had begun as a rather frivolous pursuit had, within a remarkably short time, developed into an obsession as the deeper he delved, the more his beliefs were confirmed. He had carried out midnight vigils in reputedly haunted houses, explored ancient sites purportedly plagued with 'malign forces' and had descended into the depths of the unhallowed and lonely places where none in their right minds dared venture. In the course of such undertakings he had come face-to-face with otherworldly things that most were mercifully unaware of; things that could shatter a weaker man's sanity with comparative ease.

"Well, all I can say is I'm glad I've had my lunch," commented his friend and colleague, Doctor Nigel Dexter, after having looked at the thankfully rather grainy and edited photograph which accompanied the short newspaper article which was titled: *Man's partially devoured corpse found in big cat enclosure at London Zoo*. "What a terrible way to go." He handed the newspaper back. "I take it you consider this death to be linked with the others?"

Mason nodded. "When was the last time anyone was mauled to death by a lion in London?" He returned the newspaper to the desk nearby and sat back, interlacing his long fingers, waiting for an answer.

"Has there ever been one?" Dexter asked after a brief pause.

"There have been two," came Mason's immediate reply. "At least, two which besides yesterday's have been recorded. The first was in the summer of 1854 when a lion-tamer was killed at a travelling circus in Hyde Park. The second occurred sixty years ago in 1911 when a private owner was killed by one of his pet felines long-considered docile…until it went berserk," he added with a grim smile. "Why anyone would want to keep such creatures in their houses is beyond me, but there we are."

"So I take it that you're ruling out suicide? That seems to be the angle the police are taking and from the details in the article—"

"I'd have thought that you had been in this business long enough by now to know a cover-up when you see one," Mason interrupted. "Yes, the police *may* believe this to be an act of suicide, and it may well be for the best if they continue to do so, but I think that when looked at in the light of the other so-called tragic accidents one can detect a pattern emerging. And to be honest with you, it's one that makes my skin crawl."

"You still think it's to do with him, don't you, with Zegrembi?" The very mention of the name sent a shudder through Dexter and for a moment he was certain that the light in the room dimmed slightly.

Mason said nothing, thinking, bringing his palms together and up to his face as though in prayer. For the past thirty years he had studied everything that had been written regarding the infamous diabolist, Nicholas Zegrembi, otherwise known as 'The Devil's Chosen'. What he had learned had frequently brought him to the brink of madness and it had been with only the greatest level of willpower and self-restraint that he had persevered in his unholy research. According to what he had unearthed—literally, in some cases—Zegrembi had been a leading Seventeenth Century occultist, a practitioner of the Dark Arts who had risen from an obscure mid-European background to become one of only a few to reach the rank of Ipsissimus. In 1663 he had written the infamous *Zegrembi Manuscript* which supposedly contained formulae for inter-dimensional travel and such blasphemous grimoires as *Ahrimanes Omnipotae* and Diablere—age-worn, Latin versions of which were in Mason's personal collection. Zegrembi was also credited with having fashioned numerous demonic artefacts; rare items of unearthly jewellery which possessed sorcerous powers. In 1666 he was known to have been active in London, masterminding a campaign of terror and spearheading an anti-Christian movement all with the aid of the numerous cultists he had recruited to his foul cause. This had resulted in widespread murder and mayhem as well as the desecration and destruction of several churches. Having escaped from the conflagration of the Great Fire, which, privately, Mason put down to the Devil-worshipper's instigation, his last known whereabouts were recorded as having been in a small Cornish hamlet known as Torpoint. According to the rather scant accounts, Zegrembi still retained a few fanatical followers and he continued with his Satanic and necromantic rites in the burial ground on top of the aptly-named Witchmoon Hill, uttering the most terrible curses on the inhabitants of Torpoint and there was talk of inhuman shapes seen moving among the nearby ring of standing stones around the time of the full moon and especially on All Hallows Eve. Soon, his activities had drawn a patrol of witch-hunters who been appointed by the crown. A band of them, led by the local vicar, set a trap, ambushing the demonologist and his unholy acolytes. And yet, employing his dark powers once more it was claimed Zegrembi had escaped from imprisonment and ultimately from being burnt at the stake, leaving nothing of his presence but a chalked pentagram on the stone floor of his cell.

"But why? Why him for God's sake? Surely he's been dead for over three hundred years?" There was a detectable note of dread in Dexter's questioning; a slight wavering of his voice.

"*Dead?*" Mason removed his hands from his face and presented the other with a thin smile. "Who's to say whether he's dead or not? His body was never found. And, as we both know from past experience, even if the body no longer exists that is not to say that he can longer exert his will, turning it to malign purpose. There are passages contained in the *Diablere*, explicit incantations, which deal with such matters. I've no doubt whatsoever that Zegrembi still exists, in spirit form, where, thankfully, his powers are greatly reduced."

"And yet you fear that he may return in physical form?" Dexter leaned forward in his chair.

Mason tapped the desk, cogitating, drawing his cheeks in further, giving his face the appearance of a barely flesh-covered skull. "Ex actly. It's a fear I've had for many years and one which I have rarely spoken of. It's because of this fear that I've been forever vigilant, keeping my eyes open for anything which may portend Zegrembi's return. I had all but resigned myself to discovering something like this in the papers."

"I remain confused," Dexter replied. "Why should a man being killed by lions have any bearing on the return of a three hundred year old warlock?"

"Think, man!" Mason urged. "Tie that death in with the previous deaths I've brought to your attention. The decapitated body found outside Southwark Cathedral; the unfortunate victim hanged from Tower Bridge; the body found burnt beyond all recognition in St. James' Park." Noting the somewhat confused look on his associate's face, Mason continued: "You must be blind not to see the connection for not only were all of these acts of murder…or perhaps I should say *sacrifice*…committed on the nights of the full moon but they're all—"

"I've got it," Dexter interrupted. "Martyr's deaths!"

Mason nodded. "Exactly. Death by beheading, hanging, immolation and being thrown to the lions. All means by which the saints of old met their ends."

"And…and these victims?" began Dexter. "How exactly are these deaths related to Zegrembi? Do you think that he's directly responsible or do you think that someone is committing them in order to restore him back to life?"

"The latter. Without doubt."

"Good God! They must be insane!"

"Insane, misguided, fanatical…or perhaps cursed, compelled to carry out this foul deed; ensorcelled by a power they're unable or perhaps unwilling to resist, that's assuming of course that it is but one individual. It could just as feasibly be a cult, one dedicated to restoring Zegrembi to life." Sprightly, for his age, Mason got to his feet. "It's up to us to thwart their diabolical intentions, for we alone know what is transpiring and that, my friend, puts us both in something of a dangerous position. I've no doubt that whoever is overseeing this is themselves possessed of formidable dark powers."

"But, where to start and how long do you think we have before—?"

"Before this hellish deed reaches its culmination?" Mason sharply interjected. He paced around for a few moments, thinking things through; assimilating the clues that he had gathered and deliberating on all that he knew. Whoever was responsible for this had left a trail of darkness and murder in their wake and there seemed little to go on besides pursuing the routine avenues of investigation which at the moment befuddled the police, leading only to dead ends. Four horrible murders had taken place and he was convinced he knew the connection between them. He was equally certain that, in a month's time there would be a further atrocity and that this would be the final one. Five, because that was the number of the diabolist—five points on the pentagram. All of the resurrection spells he had studied frequently made reference to that number. "In answer to your first question, I think our first place of investigation should be Torpoint itself, see if we can find any clues as to what exactly happened there three centuries ago. As to how long we have I'd say we have until the night of the next full moon."

* * * *

Torpoint no longer existed on any map. The nearest settlement of any size was the small village of Hazelwood. Two days later, after arriving by train and then taxi it was here that Mason and Dexter sought and found accommodation, obtaining rooms at the local inn, *The Saracen's Head*. It was a warm and friendly place, filled with an eclectic bunch of locals who accepted their presence welcomingly, eagerly informing them, after establishing that they were visitors from London, that life was much better out here, away from the bustling capital.

Sipping his ale, Dexter tried to settle in. He was a city man through and through, only truly content and at ease in London despite the fact that he had accompanied Mason on numerous ghostly expeditions, covering the length and breadth of the country. There was something about the reassuring presence of other people that particularly appealed to him; the need almost for human company, which, considering the many godforsaken places he had visited was not entirely surprising.

"According to what I've been able to ascertain, Torpoint, or rather what remains of it, lies some ten miles east of here. It's on the coast, and as far as I'm aware there's a reasonable road to it. We need to get someone who can provide transport there. Maybe see if there's a local taxi service." Mason looked about him, surveying the gathered patrons with some level of interest. They seemed a lively and harmless bunch for the main.

"So what do you plan to do? Are you going to ask if anyone knows anything about this place?" Dexter asked.

Mason thought things over for a moment. It did seem the logical thing to do. After all, if anyone had any information regarding Torpoint, then surely it would be someone who lived reasonably close by. It was really just a case of picking a good moment.

Half an hour later, having now finished their drinks, opportunity came knocking, when the landlord came over and sat down at their table. He was a big man, chubby cheeked, his face flushed so much it almost matched his bright red sideburns. "Well gentlemen, I do hope you enjoyed your drinks and if there's anything I can do for you while you're staying here please let me know. We try and make visitors feel comfortable. Now, I don't suppose you'd like a meal or perhaps more drinks?"

"We'll certainly be eating," answered Mason. "However, I have a question or two that I would like to ask. My friend and I are historians working for a university in London," he lied, "and we're currently researching lost Cornish villages."

"Lost Cornish villages?" replied the landlord excitedly. "Well in that case, you'll have to pay a visit to Torpoint. It's not far from here."

"Torpoint?" Mason sat back, playing the ignorant. "I've heard the name before. What can you tell me about it?"

"Well," began the landlord, "there's some that say it's a bad place. There's not much left there…only ruins. Ghosts and wild dogs too, if you believe some of the stories. It used to be a fairly thriving community. Mind you, that's going back several hundred years or so. What exactly happened to the people there I couldn't tell you, however there's always been a mystery about the place. As I said, most of it's now in ruins but I believe that the old castle building's still standing, well parts of it at any rate."

"Intriguing. Sounds exactly like the kind of place we should visit."

"I take it you came by car?"

"Taxi. We got one at the railway station."

"Hmm. Then getting to Torpoint isn't going to be easy." The barman ground his front teeth together. "Morgan there," he waved a hand towards a rather ratty-looking man with a cloth cap who was playing darts, "might be prepared to give you a lift for a couple of quid. I'd say he's probably the only one hereabouts who'd willingly go out there. It's got a rather bad reputation and many of the locals just won't go there."

"Would you be willing to have a word with your friend? Obviously we'd generously reimburse him for the trouble," queried Mason.

"Why certainly." The barman got to his feet and headed over to the man called Morgan. After a brief chat, he returned, a rather downcast look on his face. "Unfortunately, it seems that he's not willing to go out there himself. However, for some cash up front, he's prepared to loan you his car."

Mason reached into his jacket pocket and removed his wallet. "Will ten pounds be sufficient?"

"That'll be fine. I'll see to it that the car's waiting for you in the morning. Now then, you mentioned you'd like something to eat. I've got some lovely rabbit and ale pie if you fancy that."

* * * *

It was a dark and dreary morning, with frequent rain showers and heavy gales gusting in from the sea and the drive to Torpoint, in their rented car, was proving to be more of an experience than either Mason or Dexter had hoped for. The vehicle itself would no doubt be classed as un-roadworthy, both the steering and the brakes nowhere near as good as they should be, making the driving both difficult and hazardous. The road itself, with no other traffic on it, was long and winding, seemingly stretching for much further than the ten miles they had thought. In places, it dangerously neared the cliff edge, prompting Dexter to slow down drastically in order to cautiously negotiate his way forward.

The scenery they were passing was wild, unpopulated and filled with an atmospheric menace, which pressed down on them with an almost tangible, malevolent presence. Tors and the occasional lightning-blasted tree stood forlornly on the bleak horizon.

"That's weird," commented Dexter, looking into his rear-view mirror.

"What's that?"

"There appears to be a strange mist gathering behind us. I'd almost go as far as to say that it's following us."

Mason turned in his seat. Some two hundred yards distant he could see the wispy, cloud-like formation. It didn't require too much imagination to believe that it *was* advancing after them. There was something about it which lacked normality.

"There's a hill up ahead. Could that be Witchmoon Hill?"

Mason turned in his seat once more in order to look in the direction they were travelling. "Yes, I think it must be," he answered.

Before them, a mile or so distant, the hill rose from the flat, unwelcoming moorland, dominating the landscape. So many of the legends associated with this place seemed to have that dark ridge as their focal point and almost certainly there was a basis in fact for them. Just visible on the rounded summit he could make out the circle of standing stones; tall, carven monoliths whose origin had been lost in antiquity although it was certainly far older than the village, whose own history was far from short. Mason knew that the stones were certainly prehistoric in nature, belonging to a Neolithic culture, one which had undoubtedly practised bloody human sacrifices. According to the research he had done prior to coming out here, it appeared that the measurements and motions of the celestial bodies had nothing to do with this archaeological monument, suggesting that its origins and indeed function were far more horrific in origin.

They drove on for a few more minutes, thankfully noting that the lingering fog seemed to be holding back. Nevertheless, it was gloomy outside, despite the fact that it was now mid-morning.

"I don't know exactly where we should begin our search," commented Dexter. "As we were told, most of it's in ruins." He brought the car to a halt and switched off the engine. He looked at his companion. "What do you suggest?"

"I'd like to see if we can find the dungeon in which Zegrembi was imprisoned," answered Mason. He opened the passenger door and got out. "Don't forget to bring the torch, I've no doubt we're going to need it." He then went and opened the boot, removing a small black briefcase.

Together the two of them wandered among the decrepit buildings, most of them little more than heaps of rubble and timbers. It was clear that Torpoint had never been a particularly large settlement, contrary to what their informant had told them. In places it appeared that several of the houses had fallen into the sea, tumbling away with the erosion of the nearby cliff edge. Whether due to the ominous weather or to the wicked history associated with this village, an evil aura pressed down on them, smothering them almost in its foul embrace. There was no doubt this place was cursed. Occasionally, Mason would abruptly stop, listening, straining his senses as though trying to detect something unworldly.

Dead leaves swept by in the growing wind. Some whirled into small, seemingly living, tornadoes, the sound of their rustling uncanny, as though nature itself had been corrupted and had found a fell voice in this dreadful place.

Mason raised a hand, signalling his companion to a halt upon noticing an ancient building, perhaps a church of some kind, raised on higher ground, over to their right. He looked around at the grim ruins, his eyes taking in the collapsed walls, the three broken arches, the numerous leaning pillars. The slopes around the foreboding structure were of deep-toned greys—growths of hawthorn and jutting headstones making up the darkest patches. From this distance, he could see signs of ancient statuary; tortured shapes resembling surrealistic figures, misshapen heads and limbs twisted towards the looming edifice like a frozen tableau of anguished souls.

The sky darkened further.

"Good God, what a place." Dexter was looking around him, wide-eyed. There was something here, an otherworldly presence, something demonic that had leached into the very brickwork of the building before them. "It's almost as though the dead are watching our every step, railing against this trespass. I take it you can feel it too?"

"The Evil One is with us, make no mistake of that," Mason murmured. "It would appear that Zegrembi's unholy influence still taints these ruins." He put his briefcase down for a moment, reached into a jacket pocket and removed two small crucifixes. "Take this," he said, handing one over to his friend.

Stepping around several heaps of tumbled wall, they soon came to the first of thirty or so age-worn steps leading up to the sepulchral ruin. The wind gusted, lifting a russet sheet of leaves, which, for a moment, seemed to rise above them like a patchwork phantom. Even as they were about to react, an abrupt change in the wind dissipated the insubstantial menace.

Warily, they continued up.

Silhouetted against the dark and angry sky, they could now discern that the entrance was flanked on either side by tall, emaciated, bat-winged demons and although not true caryatids it was clear that the architect had fashioned them in this sense, incorporating them into the arch. The double doors which provided access had long been destroyed—one lying, smashed, on the ground, the other leaning at an angle—permitting them to see that the shadowy interior appeared to be ruined as well. Small, stone, bat-like gargoyles perched on the corners of the curiously Gothic-styled architecture, their grins and sly looks particularly unnerving.

The wind was picking up strength at an unnatural pace. Unhealthy-looking black clouds sped in from the sea as the atmosphere became laden with menace. There was an almost tangible wickedness in the wail of the wind, as though each chill gust carried with it the laments of all of those who had suffered because of Zegrembi's dreadful zealotry.

"You're going to be needing your torch soon." Mason shivered as the leaves rose up and whipped at the stonework with the fervour of a flagellant and a cold sweat dampened his forehead. Instinctively, he gripped his crucifix a little tighter. Whether it had the strength to combat the evil powers he knew to be here was something he was certain would soon be put to the test. Crossing the threshold, he stepped inside, Dexter with his switched on torch close beside him.

The chamber was cold, both men's breath now visible and, despite the gale raging outside, it was unnaturally quiet, the howls of the wind strangely muffled as though they belonged to another world; another time. Detritus that had fallen from the ceiling now covered the floor. At one end, on the fringe of their torchlight, they could discern a dark opening; the beginning of a flight of stone steps descending into the darkness,

Dexter gulped nervously. "I know we've been in several places like this before, Jeremiah, but I don't mind admitting to you that I'm scared." A stifling fear and apprehension grew within him.

"If it's any consolation, so am I." Mason tried in vain to repress a shudder and keep his tone even. "We've come this far, we have to see what's down there." Despite the illumination provided by the torch it remained shadowy, almost as though the dark was malignly reaching out to extinguish the light and he could not shake off the feeling that they were being watched. That there were eyes, evil and scheming, peering out at them from the lightless corners of the ruined interior. He tried not to think of the unholy revels and blasphemous profanities that must have taken place around here in the past centuries. Was it down there, in that unhallowed, Stygian dungeon, little more than an oubliette, that Zegrembi had been incarcerated and from which, if rumour held true, he had escaped utilising his sorcerous powers? Would any trace of his passing remain to be discovered? That was both his hope…and, if he were honest, his greatest fear. Yet if they were to find any clue as to who was attempting to resurrect him, this had to be one of the logical places to begin their search.

The steps were narrow and tortuous, the walls dank and dripping with moisture. Dexter went first, his torch only feebly managing to chase away the clinging shadows. There was a dreadful, charnel smell emanating from below; the gut-churning stench of age-old catacombs and the long-dead, making both men think that perhaps this was leading to some kind of burial tomb as opposed to a subterranean cell. On two occasions, Mason almost tripped.

"This is it," said Dexter upon reaching the bottom. He panned the torch around the small chamber. The remains of a rusty, metal gate hung open, having fallen from its hinges.

It was, as Mason had anticipated, a dungeon cell, low-ceilinged, no larger than seven or eight feet square. There was a tangible horror about the enclosed space; an otherworldly eldritchness that reached out from the un-lightable corners to grasp at them; to drag them into the dark abysses that yawned in the furthest reaches of this unnatural place. Something *alien* had occurred here, something that defied all natural scientific laws.

"Is it me or is it getting colder?" Dexter asked nervously, his exhaled breath visible as a smoky mist.

"There's no doubt the temperature is dropping," Mason confirmed. He held the crucifix out before him, aware that his hand was trembling.

"There's nothing to be found here," said Dexter, thinking it was now high time to get away from this abysmal place. "Let's get outside. We can take a look at that stone circle." Despite the horrible reputation linked to the ancient megaliths, he would much rather be outside than spend another moment down here. With some effort, he shook off the feeling of being entombed; bricked up within the bowels of the desecrated church. Such a death would be the worst of nightmares—abandoned and forgotten, left alone to rot in the darkness, with no one able to hear your screams.

"There's one more thing I want to do. Give me some light." Mason rested his briefcase on the cold floor and clicked it open. He rummaged around inside then took out a small leather bag.

"Is that what I think it is?" Dexter asked. He was now stood on Mason's immediate right.

"I just want to try something." Mason opened the bag and began sprinkling a fine, scintillating, grey-green powder on the floor. "The sacred mummy dust of Ibn Ghazi has the power to reveal the invisible." He scattered more of it about and, by some arcane magic, lines and cabbalistic markings that had hitherto gone unnoticed began to appear on the floor. Within no time at all both men stood staring down at the inscribed pentagram which had been instrumental to Zegrembi's escape.

"I've never seen anything like it," muttered Dexter. "Admittedly there are some sigils I'm aware of, but—"

"Some of these words of power are ancient; pre-dating those found in the many grimoires that would have been available to Zegrembi," Mason interjected. "There are several symbols that are undoubtedly Sumerian in origin. All of this reinforces my belief that Zegrembi was no mere Seventeenth Century warlock but rather a fiend—a demon—in human form. As such, it is imperative that we prevent whoever it is that is seeking to bring him back."

For a moment, Dexter was entranced, spellbound, his eyes fixed on the pentagram. With a mental effort he managed to break the mesmeric hold it had on him. "Where do you think it goes?" he asked.

"It *could* lead any*where*…and any *when*. However, it is my belief that Zegrembi knew exactly what he was doing. I daresay he always planned for this eventuality. Consequently, I believe that he designed it to translocate himself to someplace where his physical shell at least would be safe. As to activating it—" Mason reached inside his briefcase and removed his copy of *Diablere*. He opened it at a marked page on which were drawings very similar to the mystical design at their feet.

"But surely you're not going to—!?" There was a strong note of alarm in Dexter's voice.

"My dear Dexter. This is the only way. Now that I've found this gateway I have to enter it, to see where it goes."

"*No!* That's too dangerous!" Dexter shook his head fiercely. "You said yourself it could go anywhere! To the bottom of the ocean...or to a distant planet many years in the past or the future. It's insane!"

"I don't believe that. Zegrembi was no fool. This is a risk I have to take. Besides, I have protection of my own. I am well acquainted with many of the warding chants used to repel the many things of the Dark."

"But—?"

"I have to do this so please don't try to stop me."

"But how will you get back?" queried Dexter. "If an elaborate ritual is required to return Zegrembi..."

"Zegrembi has been gone for three hundred years. I intend to be gone for only an hour, maybe less. By reversing the formulae contained in the passages—"

"It's madness, Jeremiah. Suicidal lunacy." It was so cold now that Dexter found himself shaking all over. He was deeply worried that if his friend went through with this ill-thought out plan then he would never see him again.

"You must trust my judgement on this. I will not be gone long. If, however, I don't return—"

"Don't talk like that!"

"Even now, the pentagram is fading," said Mason, looking down. Briefcase in hand, he stepped into the middle of it. "If I don't return then it will be up to you to prevent Zegrembi's Second Coming. Inform the police. Do whatever you feel necessary to stop him." He extended a hand which Dexter shook. In a clear voice, he began to recite the incantation required to open the gateway.

There was still time for Dexter to intervene; to forcibly drag the other clear if need be. He felt powerless, unsure as to what to do for the best. Part of him was hoping that nothing would happen, but he had seen enough over the years to know that was not going to be the case. He was only dimly aware of his friend's bizarre mutterings; the alien-sounding pronunciations and occasional strange gesticulations. In the end, he just stood there, transfixed as Mason vanished.

✦ ✦ ✦ ✦

"Well, it would appear that something is wrong with the circle...or perhaps the incantation. Although I'm certain my pronunciation was correct." Mason gazed about him. His surroundings had not changed in the least. Despite his feeling of disappointment, perhaps that was for the best. "Ah well, at least—" He stopped.

Dexter was shaking his head, moving away.

"Can you...?" Mason waved an arm. Realisation struck him instantly. The other was unaware of his presence. Either the spell had rendered him invisible or else it had projected him into some kind of temporal shift—phased him into a slightly divergent timeline.

It wasn't as though he was bodiless—in fact he could see his arms and legs, so he knew he hadn't become an ethereal spirit possessed only of awareness. However, upon trying to lift his briefcase he soon discovered that he had become partially insubstantial. Indeed, it was only on his fourth attempt that he succeeded in gaining a tangible grip. More disconcerting, however, was the way in which he was gradually sliding into the stone floor. It was only through an effort of will that he managed to regain his equilibrium, levitating back so that his shoes were level with the ground. How exactly this state of being was going to assist in the quest to locate those involved in resurrecting Zegrembi he had no immediate idea but he would have to think of something, and fast, for he had no intention of remaining in this form for any longer than was necessary.

Dexter had now gone and all was dark.

Mason concentrated, reaching out with his mind, trying to detect anything that might prove informative. At first there was nothing and yet the more he focused his attention, the more he became aware that there *was* something else. It was as though a barrier had been put in place to shield or secure that *something* from prying eyes. Doubling his efforts, his mind seemed to shudder and then there was a distinct pulling sensation as his essence was propelled by an unknown force along a tunnel of midnight blackness in which the occasional pinprick of flashing electric light appeared. The motion was unlike anything he had ever experienced and he was unsure how long it lasted—time and space distorting chaotically in this weird teleportation.

When it stopped, he found himself again surrounded by darkness—only this time there was a naturalness to it that had been noticeably missing before. Despite his semi-physicality, it seemed as though his senses had become magnified and he sensed that he was in a chamber.

Was this where Zegrembi had reappeared after 'vanishing' from his cell over three hundred years ago? If so, then it was imperative that he discovered exactly where 'here' was.

With that thought, he took several steps forward, his corporeal self returning. He could feel the solidity of the briefcase's leather handle growing in his fist and he could now detect the firmness of the floor beneath him. The conclusion he reached was that an out-of-body state was required for the actual translocation but now that he had, in effect, reached his destination, such a condition was no longer necessary.

Upon reaching a wall, Mason felt around for a light switch. After a minute of groping blindly, he found it, and flicked it down. Instant luminosity bathed the room, revealing it to be much larger than he had at first anticipated. Before him was a wall with a double door set in it. Looking over his shoulder, he was not that surprised to see a magic circle almost identical to that in which he had performed the ritual on the floor. There were no windows visible, leading him to the belief that this room was perhaps beneath ground level. The ceiling was raftered with dark, oak beams and the room possessed an aura of antiquity. In addition to the magic circle with the inset pentagram which covered the floor there were other signs that this place was used for dark rituals. Many sections of wall space were covered with cabalistic markings—some recognisable, some not. Hooded black robes hung from a rack and nearby there were several glass-fronted cabinets containing candlesticks, chalices, silver daggers, skulls and other items of occult paraphernalia, much of it only too familiar to him.

Thankfully, he still retained some of his heightened awareness for he suddenly heard voices. Someone was approaching the door.

Acting quickly, Mason flicked off the light and moved into the space behind where the door would open. A moment later a key turned in the lock and the door was pushed wide. A beam of yellow torchlight spilled in.

Mason could sense the other peering into the room, eyes scanning for movement.

"Anything?" a voice, further back, called out.

"Nothing. Maybe it was just my imagination," replied the person in the doorway. "I don't think we should concern the Master anyway. Certainly not while he's at prayer."

Mason could detect an element of reluctance in the voice of who-ever it was who stood nearby, separated only by a few inches of wood. It was as though the other was fearful about setting foot inside and conducting an in-depth search. Something for which he was grateful as he doubted whether his presence here would be welcomed. Having some knowledge of the kind of people who became involved in such devilry—even those misguided fools who formed the lesser ranks—he knew that in all likelihood if he was found he would be killed, hav-ing been judged to have seen more than he should have.

The door was closed.

But whether due to his haste to get away from the room, forgetful-ness or good luck on Mason's part, the other forgot to lock it.

He waited in the darkness until all was quiet once more. He then waited a further five minutes before slowly pushing the door open. Subterfuge was not really his style, nevertheless, given the circum-stances, it was what was required. Creeping out into the corridor beyond he could see that there was another door on his left whilst straight in front of him was a flight of stone steps leading up.

Ignoring the door, he went up the steps as quietly as he could. At the top was another door which he opened carefully. He was now on a long corridor. It extended for some distance, both to his right and to his left before turning a corner. Directly in front of him was another door, slightly ajar. From beyond it a further set of stairs led up.

Crossing the corridor, he edged open the door and started up the stairs. They went up for quite some way finally ending on a narrow landing. The corridor to his left ended at a barred window and—it was dark outside. Night. Obviously there had been an alteration in time when he had shifted between the two magic circles. However, of greater surprise was what he could see rising above the rooftops outside. For there, less than a mile way, just visible, was one of the circular clock faces of Big Ben! Due to his geographical knowledge of London he reasoned that he must be somewhere in Lambeth. All he had to do now was get out and ascertain the exact address.

He paused, listening, certain that he could hear a voice coming from somewhere in the darkness over to his right. Gingerly, he moved forward. In the dimness he could make out that the walls of the cor-ridor were decorated in places with small marble busts set on plinths, housed in niches. From the ones he could see he could tell that they all depicted the same gorgon-like image of a snake-haired, angular-faced man, his eyes sharp and staring, a thick amulet around his neck. Something told him that this had to be an artistic rendering of Zegrembi.

A chamber loomed before him. The darkness inside was pervasive, like the dark of a totally eclipsed moon, giving him the unnerving impression that the area was boundless and insubstantial; a place detached from the physical world of stone and timber. Six slender pillars supported the ceiling.

Mason knew that this was an unholy sanctuary; a black chapel. For, atop a central dais, bathed in the beam of iridescent shadow, was an open, upright ornately-carved sarcophagus, before which knelt a shadowy, hooded figure. As he stood there watching, the figure rose and with a taper lit two tall black candles on either side of the stone coffin, the burning wicks giving off an oleaginous and repellent smell.

Within the sarcophagus, standing unsupported, was the well preserved corpse of Nicholas Zegrembi dressed in a full-length sable robe. But this was no withered, three hundred year old cadaver. Rather, it was that of someone only recently deceased. Candlelight flickered in the piercing, raven-like eyes, filling them with a lambent evil, making them seem alive. Long curls of jet-black hair contrasted with the skin of his lupine face which was pallid and waxen. His mouth was twisted in a sardonic grin. It was the smile of someone basking in their own brilliance—someone who knew that they had mastered death.

If Mason had a gun he would have had no hesitation in shooting Zegrembi's disciple in cold-blood in the full awareness that his act of murder could be perfectly justified in light of the chaos and the destruction the other, without doubt, had planned. He retreated back to the top of the stairs. There was little more he could here. Once he got out he would inform the police—tell them that a murder had been committed. Anything to attract their presence.

It was as he was searching for the way out that a heavy hand clamped down on his left shoulder...

* * * *

"Where are you taking me?" Mason asked. He had sat in silence, staring out of the car window as the lights of London dwindled away. Beside him, on the rear seat, sat a large man dressed in a dark suit, a gun in his hand.

"All in good time," replied the driver.

Mason sat back. He had never felt so helpless. After his capture he had been interrogated and imprisoned. He had been threatened with violence although none had been used on him.

Soon they were out in the countryside. Turning off the main road, the driver took the car along a much narrower route. Although it was dark outside, Mason detected the shadows of trees that ringed around them and from his reasonable knowledge of the area he guessed they were venturing into Epping Forest.

Through a break in the trees, the black, voluminous clouds parted revealing the bright, full face of the moon. Mason's heart leapt. It just wasn't possible. There was no credible means by which the best part of a month had elapsed since his decision to travel to Torpoint. Upon being apprehended by the followers of Zegrembi he had only been locked up for three days. The only plausible explanation for this time-shift was surely down to his use of the magic circle. He was ruminating on this and on the possibility of escape when the car began to slow down and then came to a stop.

"Time to get out," said the driver.

The car door was opened and Mason was temporarily blinded by the bright glare of his surroundings, illumination that was provided by three powerful mobile lighting systems like the kinds found on film sets. Several other cars had been parked nearby and there were over a dozen men milling around; smartly-dressed, professional types who had become thralls to Zegrembi and his new disciple. Some of them regarded Mason coldly but most ignored him completely.

"This way."

At gunpoint, Mason was directed to a place where the trees thinned out. He was then led forward onto the pristine lawn of a stately home. Floodlights bathed the place. Over to one side a stage had been erected, part of which was obscured by a thick velvet curtain. At the far end, some seventy yards away, stood a gnarled oak tree its branches warped and twisted.

Mason gulped upon seeing the tree for there was something about it that disturbed him. Throughout his forty year study of the paranormal he had come to recognise and identify the weird and the malign in its numerous guises and he was in no doubt that this rearing growth possessed both such attributes. It was as he was staring at it that he was struck by a sudden vision of corpses hanging from its many boughs. With the abruptness with which it had appeared, the mental image vanished.

Six dark-robed men, carrying braced longbows, glided silently into view, their quivers stacked with black-fletched arrows. They took up position facing the tree.

Several unsettling minutes passed during which many more dark cowled men began to gather.

From behind the stage curtains the man who Mason knew was Zegrembi's disciple stepped forth. Who he was in actuality Mason didn't know for even throughout his period of incarceration the other had not once come to see him, leaving that to his underlings. However, given the rather opulent surroundings, he had to be a person of considerable wealth—a member of the aristocracy or a politician perhaps. It wouldn't be the first time that one of the elite had joined forces with the powers of Darkness.

And then two men emerged from the woods—a third man, bare-chested, hooded, bound and struggling held between them. They frog-marched their captive towards the tree. Another cultist came fourth carrying a length of rope.

Mason watched as the unfortunate was lashed to the tree. Sudden realisation struck him. This was to be the final sacrifice; a murder committed in the same manner as the death of Saint Edmund the Martyr.

The six archers lined up—a Mediaeval-style firing squad.

The unfortunate tied to the tree was shouting, his words muffled by the hood.

With a signal from the man on the stage the arrows began to fly. The first six missed—four falling short, the remaining two disappearing into the undergrowth. Cursing their aim, the bowmen unleashed a second volley.

Three arrows struck home.

Mason looked away. This was terrible. Barbaric.

The victim was still alive—screaming in pain.

Sadistically, the archers moved closer, nocking their arrows and shooting at will, any sense of discipline in their rank now giving way to a frenzied bloodlust. Bowstrings twanged, arrows thumped into flesh and the screaming stopped. Still they shot, peppering their victim, pinning him to the tree. It was only when they had exhausted their arrow supply that the shooting came to an end.

Clapping, Zegrembi's disciple stepped down from the stage and walked towards Mason.

Now that Mason could see him better he was shocked to see how young the other appeared. He would be surprised if he was over twenty-five. There was a darkly charismatic look to his almost cherubic features. His eyes glistened green, lynx-like. What mad compulsion had led this individual down such an evil and twisted path?

"A most entertaining display, I'm sure you'd agree." The young man smiled wickedly. "But there's something more I'd like you to see. Something I'm convinced you'll find most interesting."

Two cultists grabbed Mason and steered him forward. Forcibly, he was brought before the grisly corpse that had been transformed into a human pin-cushion. It had been effectively nailed to the tree. Sixteen arrows protruded bloodily from the slumped victim.

"I told them not to hit him in the head," complained Zegrembi's disciple. He uttered an oath before grabbing the offending black-feathered shaft, and with some effort, worked it free from the blood-soaked hood. Letting the arrow fall to the ground, he then removed the covering.

Mason found himself looking into the ravaged face of his friend and colleague, Nigel Dexter.

An explosion of despair and confusion shook him to the core. His legs weakened and his eyes glazed over.

"Your friend began to get a little too close for comfort in his investigations, Mr. Jeremiah Mason." It was the first time the other had called Mason by his name. "You may take some comfort in the knowledge that his death will enable me to complete the ritual. Watch."

Before Mason's unbelieving eyes, the man reached out with a hand and began to draw a glowing, ethereal essence from Dexter's corpse. Reaching into a pocket of his robes he removed a small brass urn-like object into which he began to place the mystical extract. Once done, he gestured to Mason's restrainers to take him towards the stage where an unholy congregation had gathered at its base.

Mason was forced up the steps at the side.

The young man went behind the curtains. A minute later he reappeared. A further portion of the screen came up revealing the upright sarcophagus in which reposed Nicholas Zegrembi. "Master." He held aloft the small container. "Accept this final offering."

Like incense from a censer, the smoky substance within began to drift out, drawn towards the body in the sarcophagus.

A cheek muscle on Zegrembi's face twitched. His nose sniffed the air, inhaling Dexter's offered soul.

Mason flinched. It was a horrible sight to behold—the stirring of life back into that which was, presumably, dead.

There was a mad, ecstatic look on the young man's face as he turned to his followers. "*Behold!* Our Master awakens. The summoning is complete. The waiting of three hundred years is finally at an end. Now is the time to rejoice for chaos will reign supreme."

Nicholas Zegrembi, evil personified, breathed in the last of the sacrificial smoke. Once done, he stepped free from his funerary container. He looked about him, taking in every detail and those before him with a dark, judgemental scrutiny.

His disciple dropped to his knees, at which signal the awe-struck cultists did likewise. Hands pushed Mason into a similar subservient position.

Zegrembi glared at his disciple, his raven-like eyes pecking at the other's very soul. His features twisted in rage. "*Why?* Why have you brought me back? Speak worm!"

Fear and confusion were imprinted on the young man's face. "Master. I…I," he began.

"*It is not yet the time!*" Zegrembi shouted, the hell-fires raging in his eyes. "As Satan's lieutenant, I have been elsewhere, in the nether dimensions, gathering my forces for the final assault on Christ and his grubby, mundane creed. Through your untimely intervention my plans are now in disarray. I had an army unlike any ever amassed, ready and waiting. And now…*this*." Mockingly, he waved an encompassing hand at the dark robed congregation, clearly unimpressed.

"I beg your forgiveness. I sought only to—"

"*Silence!*" Zegrembi pointed a finger, narrowed his eyes and the other clutched his chest before keeling, lifelessly, over. He regarded Mason, a cold smile creasing his face. "I sense in you a certain wisdom that was clearly lacking from that other. You may be old, but I can prolong your life." His eyes became mesmeric pools. He reached out a hand. "Join with me and, at the appointed hour, together we will preach the religion of fear; the doctrine of the damned."

Mason's mind screamed as he found himself drowning in the ebon pits of Zegrembi's eyes. Hellish, apocalyptic visions of flame and destruction swept through his mind. Demonic, shadowy entities screamed and howled and there was blood everywhere. Under a dark, nightmarish sky he saw winged monstrosities swooping over the burning ruin of Saint Paul's cathedral. Plumes of dark smoke rose over the many churches in the capital. Giant tentacles erupted from the River Thames as it frothed and bubbled like a putrescent ichor. The Houses of Parliament were festooned in a grotesque, seaweed-like growth. The terrible images went on and on, battering down his will until his sanity was shattered.

Zegrembi regarded Mason with satisfaction. "I must now return. At this hour, on this day, thirty-three years from now you will bring me back."

Shaking the terrifying phantasmagoria from his eyes, Mason, thirty-three years younger, got to his feet. He nodded reverently to the figure before him, knowing what had to be done.

DEATH AFTER DEATH

"I'm going to take you back
to a time before you were born."

"Darling, whatever's the matter? You look awful."

Anthony Harris rubbed at his bloodshot eyes and tried to focus on his wife who was seated at the kitchen table. This was the third morning that week he had woken up screaming. He now stood wobbling slightly, his face pale and sickly-looking. His hair was wild and he was still dressed in his pyjamas. He cursed as a barefoot came down painfully on a discarded plastic toy.

One year old Alfie Harris let out a bleat of laughter from where he sat next to his mother and waved his arms, accidentally knocking over a bottle of milk.

"Are you—?" Pauline Harris got to her feet.

"Oh my God!" Unsteadily, Harris stumbled forward and managed to reach a chair. Using the table as a support, he sank down, his head in his hands. He was shaking noticeably. Twisting his face, he screwed up his eyes momentarily as if trying to shut out the memory of something that was too horrible to contemplate. Then he shook his head and took a tight grip on himself.

"What is it?" Pauline moved towards him, placing a comforting arm around his shoulder. "Was it another bad dream?"

For a moment Harris was silent. He seemed to be suffering from one of the worst hangovers imaginable. He began tugging gently at his ruffled hair. "That was the worst so far. It was…horrible"

"Let me get you a coffee." Pauline prepared to move away.

"It was so real. So bloody real…with an emphasis on the bloody. It was as though I was actually *there*. I feel as though " Harris quickly reached out for his wife's now empty cereal bowl and threw up into it. A cold shiver went through his entire body and he began to shake convulsively. Wiping strands of sick and spit from his quivering lips, he slumped against the table, his breath coming out in great wracking heaves.

"I'll phone Doctor Yates."

Now that he had been sick, Harris felt marginally better. "No… that won't be necessary. Besides, I've an appointment with him this afternoon."

He leaned back in his chair and began to regulate his breathing. The sight and smell of his fresh vomit in the bowl almost triggered a second bout of nausea but he managed to force it down. "I'll have that coffee though. Black and extra strong.

"Sure." Pauline gathered up the bowl and made for the sink. After disposing of the vomit and rinsing clean the bowl, she began boiling the kettle.

Harris tried his best to smile at his son but succeeded only in a grimace. He knew he had to keep down the horrible images that had plagued him in the last few minutes before waking. The very thought of the vileness which his subconscious had conjured in his brain sent a further jolt through his body. He felt like tilting his head back and screaming to the ceiling. For in his nightmare he had seen himself looking down on his own torn-apart body. His broken, severed limbs lay scattered around his blood-drenched torso and yet he could see he was still alive, his mouth working madly, yelling insanely, his eyes filled with blood and terror.

"Will you be all right going to work this morning?" Pauline asked, pouring his drink. She came over and rested the steaming cup by her husband's elbow.

"Yes. I think so. Besides, it's only a half-day." Harris worked as a technician at a large industrial research centre some ten miles away. "I'll finish this drink, then I'll go and have a shower."

"Do you feel up to having any breakfast?"

"Just some toast." Harris sipped at his coffee. He was trying to put things into perspective; to come to terms with his horrendous vision and to deal with the insanity of what he had witnessed some half an hour previously. It was just a dream—a particularly vivid and nasty dream—but a dream nonetheless. He pinched his hand, feeling the pain register, ensuring to himself that this was reality. It had been unlike anything he had— He stopped himself. There had been something once…something similar. But that had been long ago. Very long ago.

A fresh bout of confusion and madness threatened to seize him as he sought to untwine the dark vines now growing in his mind.

"Here's your—" Pauline stopped, seeing the ghastly look on her husband's deathly pale face. "I'm going to phone Doctor Yates right away." She put down the plate on which were four slices of buttered toast and raspberry jam and made for the hall.

"No!" Harris looked up. "I'll be all right. Honestly. All I need is—" The sight of the lumpy dark-red jam almost triggered another bout of sickness. He stared at the sticky preserve, half-expecting it to suddenly liquefy and seep over the plate. He turned away quickly. Gulping, he staggered like a cripple to his feet.

"Take my advice and go back to bed. I'll phone your boss and say you won't be—"

"I have to go in today. There's an important job on this morning."

"Don't be a fool, Anthony! You're sick. Anyone can see that. I'm sure that Mr. Burgess will be very understanding. It's not as though you've ever missed a day before."

"I...I'm feeling better already." It was a lie but Harris knew he had to say something. It was imperative that he went to work today. "Maybe I'll feel better after a quick shower." Ignoring his wife's protestations, he somehow made his way out of the kitchen and climbed the stairs to the bathroom.

* * * *

Forty minutes later, after Harris had showered, dressed and drunk two more strong coffees, he got in his car, ready to go to work.

It was a fine morning, the bright early Spring sunlight warm and pleasant.

He switched on the car engine and put it into reverse. He backed out of the drive and turned on to the main road.

Mercifully, he was now genuinely feeling better. Now that the initial shock was fading, dissolving from his mind, he felt that he could properly tackle the day ahead. He focused on driving, pleased to have something grounding to divert his troubled mind. The details of the nightmare were now hazy; little interconnected pieces of horror that were gradually evaporating—a troubling smoke that was becoming a mist. If he managed to stop thinking about it perhaps it would soon vanish completely. In time, it might become something he could laugh at.

He settled back in his seat.

Houses flashed past as he stepped on the accelerator. Soon he was out in the countryside. He turned on the car radio. It was tuned to a classical music station and some loud, operatic piece, filled with gusto and bravura, blasted forth. It was not anything he had ever heard before but it was rousing stuff all the same.

The music finished in time for the eight o'clock news.

After the broadcaster had introduced himself he went straight into the main story

"Police were this morning called to an address in Croydon where they discovered the dismembered body of a man. The butchered remains of forty-four year old Anthony Harris were found…"

A shockwave blasted through Harris' mind. His hands left the steering wheel and the car swerved dangerously. Raging thoughts crashed through his brain. Fear was a black cloud about him, choking and suffocating, stifling his breath and threatening to stop the thudding of his heart. At the last moment he regained control of the car and steered it back from disaster. Through the insanity, he managed to take in the closing news item.

"…the deceased's wife, thirty-five year old Pauline Harris, has been taken into custody. The police are not looking for anyone else in connection with the grisly murder. In other news, the supermarket giant—"

Heart thumping, Harris switched the radio off and brought the car to a stop. He sat there, gazing absently through the windscreen, his fingertips gently patting his damp forehead. His brain was rambling, descending through a veritable host of dark and senseless possibilities, trying to pull an answer from the irrational thoughts and half-formed ideas that ran chaotically through his mind.

Was he on the verge of going insane?

His surroundings darkened as clouds gusted in from the north. Everything about him was suddenly ominous, filled with a dread that was impossible to overcome. It was as though dark claws were reaching for him, tearing into his psyche, attempting to rip his very being to pieces.

"No!" he screamed, bringing his fists down heavily on the dashboard. "It can't be!" He looked up at his reflection in the rear-view mirror and for a second he was convinced that the man that looked back at him from the reflective surface was someone other than he.

Then his familiar visage reappeared. There was a haunted look in his eyes and perspiration sheened his skin.

There came a sudden rap on the side window.

Harris jumped in his seat. He turned and saw a young police constable gazing in at him. He wound down the window.

"Good morning, sir. I take it everything's all right?"

Harris nodded. It was the best he could do at the moment.

"I must say your driving back there was a little erratic. You're very lucky there was no oncoming traffic when you veered across the road."

"I...I had a fright. That's all," replied Harris.

"A fright?"

"Yes...I've not been sleeping too well of late and I—" Harris paused. "Do I look all right to you?"

The police constable stood confused. "Why...yes."

So at least I'm not lying chopped-up in a black body bag in the back of an ambulance on the way to the morgue.

Harris let out a long sigh of relief. "Well, I do apologise for my driving back there, constable. I assure you it won't happen again. A momentary lapse, that's all."

"Very good. Seeing as there was no harm done, I suppose I'll let you off this time but please be more careful in future." Satisfied, the police constable prepared to move off.

"There hasn't been anything major reported in town this morning, has there?" Harris asked. "No, well, murders or anything?"

"Not that I'm aware of, sir." The policeman looked at him curiously. "Why do you ask?" There was a touch of suspicion in his tone.

"I thought I heard something on the radio. That's all." Harris smiled and tried to look more normal than he felt. "Maybe it was somewhere else. Well, if it's all right with you, constable, I'd best be getting to work and I can assure you I'll take it more carefully."

* * * *

That news item had been nothing more than his feverish imagination playing tricks on him, he tried to convince himself as he pulled into the research centre. He drove up to the main checkpoint and fumbled with his security pass. Slowly the barrier was raised and he turned off the avenue, heading for the staff car park.

It was then, just as he was about to park the car, that he felt a peculiar tingling in his wrists It was as though a hundred hot little needles were pricking into his skin. He stopped the car in a parking bay and rolled up his sleeves, alarmed to see that both forearms, from about halfway down to the wrists, were now covered with a mysterious blue-red weal. Fear surged through his brain as he stared in puzzlement and horror, not knowing just what had happened. Was it some kind of allergic reaction? He felt like screaming. "What the hell?" he asked himself as, removing his wristwatch, he began to rub at the strange marks in the vain hope that he could wipe them away.

Things were now becoming very sore. There was a tightening sensation and he began to lose all feeling in his hands. He tried to flex his fingers but found it excruciating.

Biting down his pain, and using his shoulder and his elbow, Harris somehow managed to open the car door. He had no sooner clambered out when he felt his arms being raised as though they were being pulled by invisible ropes. He no longer had any control over his own body. Matters were made worse when he felt a similar sensation around his ankles. There was an agonising squeezing.

For a fleeting second he was lifted a couple of inches off the ground.

A car door slammed shut nearby.

Harris' feet landed back on the tarmac.

"Morning, Anthony!" called out a deep voice. "I take it you're all set for the testing of the new—" Edward Burgess, the chief director of the site and Harris' boss came striding forward, fixing his glasses to his face. "Are you feeling all right? You look a little peaky, if you don't mind me saying."

Harris looked worse than peaky. He looked downright awful but at least he was back on the ground and the pain in his wrists and ankles had all but vanished. The marks on his arms were still plainly visible. They were now beginning to turn an ugly, bruised blue-black.

"There's a nasty bug going around just now." With no further talk, Burgess started for the main buildings.

Harris watched him go. Had the man not seen what had just happened? And as for the discolouration on his arms—surely he would have noticed.

Now that the pain had finally gone, he found himself getting dazedly back into his car. Taking in some deep breaths, he tried to regain some element of composure. As a scientist, he had always sought to explain the world about him in a clinical, logical manner. Yet he knew that there was something seriously wrong with him. For even if he had just imagined all that had happened to him so far this morning, there was no denying the reality of the marks on his arms. They stood out livid and stark.

Yet his boss had failed to see them.

He examined them again. He ran his fingertips over the wounds, feeling the rough abrasions on the damaged skin. If this was all some kind of delusion, perhaps brought on by a sickened mind, then why were they tangible?

Confused, he opened the car door, stuck a trousered leg out and rolled up the hemline, not particularly surprised to see the same red raw weal just above his sock.

That was it. Coming swiftly to the conclusion that he had to seek professional help, Harris pulled his leg back inside, slammed the car door and drove off. His determination to get to work seemed ludicrous to him now. His appointment with Doctor Yates was scheduled for later that afternoon but surely what he was experiencing called for immediate assistance.

A disturbing sensation of impending disaster began to take hold of him, stirring deep in the vaults of his mind. There had been times in the past when a kind of warning bell had rung, alerting him to danger long before it actually materialised and he knew from instinct never to ignore it. The thought made him grip the steering wheel tighter, almost convulsively, his muscles tautening themselves of their own volition.

With a conscious mental effort, he forced himself to think clearly. He had to put things into some kind of perspective. He was undoubtedly sick; suffering from some mental disorder. The sooner he could be diagnosed by an expert and given proper medication the better.

The traffic up ahead had slowed down. A tailback had formed and Harris could see the cause—a slow moving tractor. However, he failed to notice the sign on the verge informing motorists of the hedge trimming taking place five hundred yards ahead.

The country road was narrow and full of hidden twists and turns which made overtaking treacherous. Seizing their opportunity, the two cars ahead of him pulled out and made the manoeuvre, each nipping back into lane before a sudden bend.

Harris edged his car forward so that he was now directly behind the tractor. He could see the mud being kicked up by its huge, deep-treaded tyres and even with the windows down he could smell the cow dung it emitted. Small clouds of black, noxious exhaust fumes belched out.

Tattered fragments of the nightmare were returning unbidden and unwelcome to Harris' memory. Terror raced through his body and there was a dull throbbing at the back of his temples, behind his eyes. Wiping a sheen of damp sweat from his forehead, he shifted the car to the right slightly, gauging the road ahead, wondering if he could overtake.

There were no turnoffs and he knew that in all likelihood he would be behind this frustratingly slow-moving vehicle for a good time for its driver showed no sign of pulling over. To make matters worse there were now two cars behind him and in his rear-view mirror he could see the impatient look of the motorist following him.

Harris was a confident driver and under different circumstances he would have probably overtaken by now, but today things were very different. There was something holding him back, a heightened awareness perhaps of his own mortality.

The driver behind hooted his horn.

"Okay! Okay!" Harris veered out further. The road ahead looked clear but he would have to be quick for there was a curve to the right coming up. Shifting gears, he decided to take his chance. He pulled out and sped forward.

Spraying a cloud of leaves and twigs and screeching like an operating saw-mill, the hedge-trimming vehicle lumbered out of a concealed farmyard entrance on his right.

The huge mechanical arm of the machine swung into view before his windscreen. A lethal blur of rotating, scything blades flashed before him.

A blast of car horns erupted in his ears.

At the last moment, Harris managed to swing the car over, narrowly avoiding a gruesome death. His heart was thumping wildly as he fought to control his vehicle. For a split-second, he saw himself lying diced and mangled; his body lacerated beyond recognition, his car windscreen smashed to pieces; the vehicle, a sundered wreck.

Then, the danger over, he stepped on the accelerator and sped off unaware that he was holding his breath until it hurt in his lungs. He heard it gasp harshly as he released it suddenly. There was a peculiar salty taste in his mouth where a thin trickle of blood was flowing from his bitten lower lip.

This was proving to be the worst day of his life but there was worse to come. Much worse.

* * * *

On the drive back Harris had decided to call in at home first, to inform his wife of his altered plans.

But she's being questioned by the police over your brutal murder, muttered an insidious little voice inside him.

Fiercely shaking his head, he pulled into his drive and parked the car. Everything was just as he had left it little under an hour ago. There were no policemen stood outside; no crime scene investigators sealing the place off with their lengths of tape.

Nerves tingling, he got out and went up to the front door. With a shaking hand, he removed his key from a pocket, opened the door and went inside. There was no sign of his wife or son which was of no real surprise for today was the day they went to her sister's on the other side of town. They would be well on their way there by now.

Taking off his jacket, Harris closed the door behind him and went into the lounge.

The domestic normality and familiarity of his surroundings were doing wonders in restoring his peace of mind. He switched on the television, sat on the sofa and waited for the local news to come on.

Ten minutes later, having heard no mention of any dismembered corpse having been found in the vicinity, he forced himself to accept that it *had* all be purely delusional. Of course it had—after all he was still here with all his limbs intact. Even the marks around his wrists and ankles had all but vanished. There was a residual puffiness and they were tender to the touch but apart from that they looked more or less normal.

It had just been a bad morning.

Still, Harris thought a stiff drink would help calm his nerves. He got up from the sofa and paced over to the drinks cabinet. There was an unopened bottle of single malt whisky which he had been keeping for his birthday but right now he thought his current need was greater. Unscrewing the lid, he poured himself a generous measure and went back to the sofa.

The first sip was heavenly. He followed with another, the raw liquor pleasantly warming the back of his throat and soothing his nerves. He leaned back and closed his eyes.

Aaaaaagggh!

A tortured scream burst from his mouth as instant, agonising pain wrenched through his entire body. The whisky glass fell from his hand on to the carpeted floor as he leapt to his feet like someone who had just been subjected to an immense electric current. The pain was intense yet fleeting and he knew that had it lasted a moment longer he would surely have passed out, such was its ferocity.

"What's happening to me?" he yelled to the empty room. "What the hell's happening to me?"

The bizarre rash was coming back to his wrists. He could see it spreading before his very eyes. The pain in his ankles now flared up again. It was as though he had been manacled by a sadistic torturer who was taking great delight in tightening his leg irons. Invisibly fettered, he somehow staggered into the hallway, the pain biting deeper with every stumble. Frantically, he reached the phone and managed to call for an ambulance. He had just finished when the pain became a dark blinding sheet of fire that tore through his body, rendering him unconscious.

* * * *

Harris' return to consciousness was slow and forced. The sensation was more than a little alarming as his mind, stimulated in part by the mental images carried over from that truly terrible nightmare, conjured up a myriad of dark, unanswered questions. There was a swirling fog inside his brain and his eyes ached. He was lying in a bed which was screened off. Disorientated and unsure of his surroundings, he panicked for a moment then sat up.

"Help! Will someone tell me where the hell I am?"

A male nurse parted the curtains and peered in. "Ah, Mr. Harris. I'll go and let the doctor know that you're awake." He disappeared as quickly as he had appeared.

Stifling the cry that threatened to burst from his lips, Harris freed his arms from the blanket, horrified to see that both wrists now had crude bracelets made of rope wrapped around them.

The curtain was pulled back on its rail and a tall, bespectacled doctor stepped into view. "Good afternoon, Mr. Harris. I'm Doctor Andrews and I'm pleased to see that you're finally awake."

Pitifully, Harris held out his arms. "Help me," he whimpered. "For the love of God, help me! Take these things off!"

Doctor Andrews walked forward uncertainly. "*What things?*"

"These ropes! They burn and I can feel them tugging at me."

"But there are no ropes."

"The pain. Make the pain go away. Please, I'm begging you!"

"Mr. Harris. Having been in touch with your treating psychiatrist, Doctor Yates, I'm of the view that the pain you claim to be experiencing is purely psychosomatic." Doctor Andrews briefly consulted a medical clipboard. "You've been X-rayed and thoroughly examined and I'm pleased to say that there's absolutely no signs of trauma to either your arms or your legs. I can also assure you that there are no ropes. Now—"

"Does...does my wife know I'm here?"

"Yes. I believe she should be along soon, but in the meantime may I suggest that you get some rest."

"I need painkillers! Give me the strongest you've got. Morphine, something like that."

"I'm afraid not." Doctor Andrews shook his head. "I don't want to prescribe a strong dose of analgesics until we can really assess the true problem here. If indeed there is one at all." He looked sceptical. After all there was no evidence to support his patient's claims. Quite the opposite in fact.

"Doctor, I woke this morning having seen my body torn limb from limb! Then something hauled me off the ground and, believe me, I'm definitely in need of painkillers. So don't you stand there and tell me there's no problem."

"I'm sorry, Mr. Harris. Now if you'll just—"

"To hell with this!" Harris swung his legs out of the bed and got to his feet.

"Please, calm down and—"

"No! I've had enough of this! If I am cracking up then I want to see Doctor Yates." Harris fought to regain control of his limbs. With difficulty, he managed to hobble his way down the ward, heading for the exit doors. They opened and he saw his wife. "Pauline," he called. "Help me get out of here! Help me get these ropes off!"

There was a grave look on Pauline's face as she rushed to assist her troubled husband.

Ignoring Doctor Andrews' pleas, they both headed out of the hospital.

* * * *

There was an excruciating agony in Harris' extremities as his wife drove down the high street, searching for somewhere convenient to park. He felt like screaming as he watched the bindings on his wrists constrict, crushing the delicate bones under the skin and cutting off the circulation to his hands. His fingers were turning blue. There was a wrenching in his shoulders and such was the severity he expected he was going to be torn limb from limb at any moment. The rending pain in his ankles was just as severe.

It was how he imagined an unfortunate being wracked would feel. That was it! He was being subjected to some form of Mediaeval torture.

Gonzalo Barabas!

The name flashed through his mind. He felt himself slipping in and out of consciousness. A dark hold came over him as the all-out agony tore through his body and the last sight he witnessed before passing out once more was of a fat, jolly-looking butcher chopping meat in a high street shop, his cleaver coming down heavily, separating the cuts of beef.

* * * *

Out of the darkness shone a pencil-thin beam of intense white light.

"Hello! Is there anybody in there?"

Harris could feel pressure on his right eyelid. He was lying flat on a low couch.

"Mr. Harris. Can you hear me? This is Doctor Yates." The words were soft and mellow, pleasing on the ear. "I'm going to give you an injection. You'll feel a little scratch."

Harris mumbled something. He felt his shirt sleeve being rolled up and then the fleeting stabbing sensation as the hypodermic pierced his skin. Thankfully, it was the only pain that registered at the moment. He felt some of his energy returning and a few minutes later he sat up, noting immediately that the ropes and marks on his arms had vanished.

"I must say you're looking better than you did ten minutes ago."

"Where's Pauline?" asked Harris, looking around.

"Your wife's gone to collect your son from her sister's but all I want you to do at the moment is relax." The psychiatrist returned to his desk. "I know that we've been over this several times before but I really think if we want to treat what's plaguing you we'd better go over it once more. So, these nightmares you've been having. When did they first begin?" He sat on the edge of a chair, a pad resting lightly on his right knee. He held a pen poised above it expectantly.

Harris stared vacantly at the ceiling for a long moment then licked his lips. "Several weeks ago."

Doctor Yates nodded and jotted something down on his pad. He eyed his patient observantly. "I see that you're constantly examining your arms. Your wife mentioned something about *ropes*."

"There were ropes fastened around my wrists."

"And…these ropes. I take it they're no longer there?"

"They've gone…for the moment. As has the pain."

"Good." Doctor Yates eased his tall body into a more comfortable position. "I take it the pain is always associated with your seeing of the ropes?"

"Not at first but it seems to be now."

"And this, shall we say physical dimension to your dreams has only come on today? No indications of this before?"

"Just this morning. It first happened when I got to work. I was lifted off the ground."

The psychiatrist's eyebrows raised. "Interesting." He scribbled something else on his pad.

"Well what is it, doctor? Am I mad? I guess I must be."

"Of course not. However, with your permission, I'd like to perform a little experiment. It's quite simple really, but it should give me an insight into your mental processes."

Harris smiled weakly. "What sort of experiment, doctor?"

"Nothing elaborate. Merely an association of words. I'm going to say a word and all I want you to do is tell me the first word that you think of. Whether or not it seems to make sense at the time is of little consequence. Are you ready?"

"Yes.

"Very well. Here's the first word…day."

"Night."

"Good."

"Eee…evil."

"Life."

"Mmm…muerte." Harris struggled as the Spanish word for *death* blurted from his mouth.

Yates sat up. "White."

"Nnnn…*negro*."

"Fear."

"Mmm…*miedo, miedo*…what's happening?" Harris exclaimed. "I don't know that word!"

"Try to relax, just say whatever comes to mind." Yates spoke calmly. "Torture."

"*Para! Para por el amor de dios!*" Harris suddenly shrieked. The room seemed to be melting and swirling in front of his eyes and the tightness was beginning in his wrists and ankles once more.

"You're safe, Anthony. Nothing is happening to you here in my office," Doctor Yates insisted gently, his voice level and with little variation in tone. "You need to speak in English. Your native tongue is English, not Spanish. Tell me what you are feeling."

Harris fought to make his eyes focus but he felt as if he was falling sideways, that the room was tipping. He could feel an intense heat and heard the sound of many people close by. The ropes were back on him and he felt himself lift off the ground, on his back. There was red, rocky sand beneath him. Sweat stung his eyes and there was blazing sunlight on his face.

Terrified, he thrashed his body from side to side and started shouting: "Anthony Harris! I'm Anthony Harris! *Me llamo Gonzalo Barabas!*" He was vaguely aware that the psychiatrist was bending over him and pulling his head round.

"Look at me, Anthony! You are here, in Croydon. It's March the twenty-ninth, 1972. Look at me!"

Harris gradually felt the sand beneath him turn to carpet. The heat faded and the pain subsided. He was lying spread-eagled on the floor of the psychiatrist's office and sweat was prickling all over his body. He tried to speak but found he was terrified at what might come out of his mouth. Painfully, he pulled himself up into a sitting position.

Doctor Yates brought him a glass of water. "Drink this and listen... no, don't talk for a minute, just listen." He brought his chair over, opposite Harris. "I believe that we are finally getting somewhere. Your speech just now, your panic as if you were in mortal danger...it all points to one thing—you are remembering a past life or perhaps I should more accurately say, a past *death*."

Harris stared at the man in confusion.

"Many people, many religions, believe that the human soul is reincarnated and lives through many different lifetimes before achieving peace. Normally, the soul has no memory of the other lives but I have heard of cases where the barrier between one life and the next becomes weak, especially if the individual in question suffered a very traumatic death. People start to have glimpses of other lives they have lived and this can bring huge problems with it."

Harris had to say something. "You can't really believe that surely? It's nonsense; religious claptrap!"

"How can you be so sure?" Doctor Yates countered. "I too was sceptical when I first heard about this concept but I've seen too many patients over the years who have had no basis for their neuroses and aberrations that can be pinpointed in their past. At least, not in their current lives. I've done my best to give them coping strategies but I've never felt satisfied. You, however..."

He looked more animated than Harris had ever seen him. "You may actually be able to access the memories of your former life and if so, can move past the trauma you experienced. The fact that you are experiencing such a strong manifestation of it shows that it needs to be acknowledged. If you do not, then it will continue to torment you."

"But this is ridiculous, impossible!" Harris protested, wiping sweat from his face.

"What was your name?" Doctor Yates suddenly demanded, grabbing Harris by the wrists and squeezing hard.

Harris gasped at the pain. "*My name?* You know my name. I'm... I'm..." He was struggling to shape the words in his mouth. There was an inner conflict taking place, a battle of wills. Inside his head he heard a chorus of voices screeching and shouting in Spanish, their words unintelligible.

Doctor Yates steered his patient back to the couch where he sat him down. He began waving his pen torch from side to side. "Focus on the light and answer my questions. Who are you?"

There was a vacant look in Harris' eyes as he began to talk. "I'm Anthony Brian Harris."

"Where were you born and in what year?"

"Retford, Nottinghamshire. 1926."

"What date?"

"April the twelfth."

"Who were your parents?"

"Jack and Betty Harris."

Doctor Yates was swinging the light faster. Back and forth. Back and forth. "You're feeling very sleepy, Anthony. Close your eyes and let your mind drift. Imagine you're falling down a long, dark tunnel, spiralling away. Down. Down. I'm going to take you back to a time before you were born."

* * * *

Spitting and cursing, Gonzalo Barabas—thief, bandit, murderer and rapist—was frogmarched through the jeering mob of spectators out into the dusty arena of the converted bullring. The noon day sun was like a furnace which struck at him without mercy, pulsing down at him in great waves of heat, burning and stinging his shirtless, freshly lashed back. With each step, the sand beneath the soles of his bare feet grew hotter. Blood from a rifle butt wound—a farewell present from one of his gaolers—trickled down the side of his rugged, unshaven face. Like a stream in a gulch, it dribbled down a furrow in his cheek, collecting on a swollen, split bottom lip. His tongue tasted it, relishing the moisture, no matter its source.

The horses were waiting; four large, powerful creatures that champed and neighed, their flanks flecked with sweat. Stout wooden yokes were being fastened to them by two uniformed men.

There was no time for fear. Fear was for the weak.

Defiantly, Barabas, his face scarred, cracked, bruised and blistered, gazed up at the fiery disc in the sky, the intense brightness burning his piercing green eyes. For a moment, he managed to discern its shimmering outline. Then he was roughly pushed forward. He fell to his knees before being hauled upright by the hair.

Half a dozen steps and then he was manhandled to the ground. The sand burned his back.

Someone was screaming and it was only after his hands had been securely strapped to the metal bars attached to the lengths of thick rope that he realised it was him. Frantically, he kicked out, landing a scuffing blow on one of his captors. Then his feet were being clamped, bound as were his hands. Out of the corner of his eye he could see the array of butchering tools spread out on the ground; knives and hatchets—bladed implements that would be called for if the horses failed to—

There was a blinding flare of agony as his body was lifted from the sand, raised by the sudden movement of the horses. Then the beasts were being whipped and the true pain began.

* * * *

Harris screamed and sprang upright. His eyes were staring wildly and sweat boiled from his face. There was a dryness in his throat and he found it hard to swallow.

Doctor Yates had stopped the pendulum-like motion of his pen torch. "Are you all right, Anthony?" he asked.

"What happened?" Harris gasped.

"Under hypnosis I successfully regressed you to a past life. You were living the last moments of a previous existence. From what I could make out it would appear that you were once a notorious Spanish criminal named Gonzalo Barabas who was sentenced to death sometime in the late-seventeenth century. The method of your execution was quartering by wild horses."

Harris got to his feet. "No! This can't be happening."

"You can't hide from your past, Anthony, no matter how much you may want to. It's all embedded here, in your brain," said Doctor Yates, tapping his temple. "You were, and to some extent still are, *Gonzalo Barabas*."

"No! This is madness!" Harris made for the door. "Complete and utter—"

"Don't fight it, Anthony. Better to accept and work through the memories."

"Never!" Harris flung the door wide and lurched out into the waiting room. "You're the one who's mad! You're the one who needs a doctor!" he shouted over his shoulder. His mind was reeling and his heart was palpitating furiously in his chest. His whole being fizzed and hummed with fear and disbelief; unable and unwilling to accept what his psychiatrist had just told him. Crashing against a door, he stumbled out into the main street.

A man walking his dog cursed as he was bumped into.

Oblivious to the strange looks he was getting, Harris staggered up the street.

You were, and to some extent still are, Gonzalo Barabas. The words preyed on his mind, fastening leech-like to his brain. With each hurried step, he could feel them gnawing away at him; the psychological pain now becoming physical once more as the sense of fugue—of separation from his own self—grew greater.

"Hello. Are you all right?"

A face he thought he knew swam into vision before his eyes.

"You're not looking too good."

His left leg buckled beneath him and he half-fell into the road, an outstretched hand reaching for the bonnet of a parked car in order to support him.

"You're not drunk are you? Come on, pull yourself together man."

Pull yourself together—something's trying to pull me apart! Unsteadily, he edged back on to the pavement.

You were, and to some extent still are, Gonzalo Barabas.

With a cry of utter horror and pain, Harris was dragged over the car bonnet. There came a terrible ripping sound and, accompanied by a thick jet of blood, his left arm was wrenched from his body.

People screamed as the limb was sent flying across the road.

The gentleman in the now blood-spattered suit who had tried to help Harris stared, wide-eyed and horror-stricken.

His yelling and screaming drowning out that of the horrified bystanders, Harris was now suspended in the middle of the road, his back horribly curved. He was beginning to unravel. There came a further tearing noise as the bones and sinews of his right arm were stretched to breaking point. Then, with a pop and a wet-sounding splatter, the limb was ruptured, torn from its socket. It went spiralling into the air, hit a shop window and, leaving a messy smear down the glass, landed on the ground whereupon a dog quickly snatched it up and ran off with it.

His arms having now been reduced to unsightly stumps of bone, blood and gristle, what remained of Harris was dragged by unseen forces down the centre of the road. Still very much alive, he felt every moment of excruciating agony as first one leg, then the other was torn from his body.

And then a darkness began to descend.

There were people standing over him, looking down in fearful, morbid curiosity. In the distance he thought he could hear the sound of an approaching siren.

"Jesus Christ! I've never seen anything like it."

"Poor bastard! His eyes are still moving!"

"Anybody know who he is?"

It was just as death finally took him that he heard the last voice.

"His name is Gonzalo Barabas. He is—or rather *was*—a wanted man in Spain." Doctor Yates looked down indifferently on the messy remains of his patient, wondering if he had finally perfected his method of murdering by past-life regression and psychological suggestion—and the occasional surreptitiously administered drug. There were a few more test subjects he was working on but this trial, as he considered it, had proved demonstrably successful. Smiling to himself with satisfaction, he turned and walked away.

THE MADNESS OF MORGENSTEIN

Welcome to the ultimate live
role-playing adventure game...

Chris Summers vomited once more into the sick-bag. He was feeling terribly queasy; the constant undulating motion of the boat having triggered a severe bout of nausea. His skin was clammy and his face was whiter than the puke-stained shirt he wore—a shirt which had been pristine when he had boarded the vessel two hours previously. Although that now seemed a lifetime ago; standing happily with his case at the dock in Lerwick, having just enjoyed a full Shetland breakfast. With that thought, he gave another violent lurch, filling the now sodden and stinking container he held weakly in his trembling hands. Through glazed eyes, he could see that many of the other passengers were likewise suffering.

Some lay flat on the carpeted floor as though dead, others were slumped at tables, moaning and groaning, their heads clasped in their hands. It was as though they had been struck down by a pestilence. All that was missing was the boils and the bleeding orifices.

"How are you faring, Summers, old boy?" Quentin Torrence asked, having just returned from the bar. By some miracle, he had weaved his way through the afflicted and maintained a steady balance, such that not a drop from the drinks on his tray had been spilled. Placing it down on the table, he took his seat.

With a paper napkin, Summers wiped the drool from his chin. "This is dreadful."

"Don't suppose you'll be wanting a bacon butty then, will you?" Torrence unwrapped one of the meat-filled rolls, peeled back the bun in order to examine its contents and then took a bite. Within a matter of seconds, he had devoured the lot and reached for the second one on the tray. He looked up, the annoying smirk of someone impervious to the surrounding suffering on his handsome, clean-shaven face. Not a hair was ruffled and his expensive lounge suit was spotless. He was tall, aristocratic and well-educated and he looked as though he could have just stepped from his Cambridge insurance-firm office. "Sure you don't want one? It's better you eat; get something to line your stomach. When I used to do a lot of cruising, back before I got divorced from Audrey, it was the first thing we were told to do whenever the waves got a bit choppy."

Summers stared blankly. "I feel as though I'm going to die."

Torrence smiled. "Don't talk crap. Try not to think about it, or even better, look out the window and focus your eyes on the horizon." He glanced at his wristwatch. "We should reach land in just under fourteen hours and I guarantee that this whole experience will just be a ghastly nightmare. You'll have forgotten about it come this time tomorrow."

"Fourteen hours?" Voiding the remnants of breakfast—an obscene coagulate of undigested mushrooms, tomatoes and bits of Lorne sausage—from his guts, Summers began to shiver. In thirty-three years of life, he could not recall having ever experienced anything as bad as this. As a successful business man, he had travelled widely. On countless flights to Europe and the United States he had endured some of the worst turbulence imaginable, even having been aboard a chartered flight that had nosedived towards the ocean before the pilot had, mercifully, regained control. However, none of it was on a par with this seemingly endless torture.

"Well, so long as you've included me in your will." Torrence took a drink of coffee, one hand on the tray to prevent it from sliding off the table. "Anyway, count yourself lucky. At least you're not as bad as Hayes."

It was only now that the name of their third companion had been mentioned that Summers realised that the occasionally obnoxious and seldom sober Irishman was not present. "Where…is he?"

"Last I saw him he was passed out on the pool table. Covered in his own filth…and we're not just talking sick. Man's a disgrace; a bloody liability if you ask me. Christ knows what you see in him."

Unwilling to respond, Summers just shook his head. He then moaned as, without warning, the boat was lifted high on the crest of a wave, the vacuum in his stomach rebelling against the sudden motion. A mental image formed in his mind of his insides seething like the turbulent North Sea they were now crossing; a constant churning, spinning, spuming, up and down movement that was far worse than any amusement park roller coaster.

"Whoa! That was a high one!" Torrence commented with some measure of glee.

"Why…didn't we fly?" Summers' words sounded pathetic; numb.

"You know the answer to that, old boy. The airport at Vágar is temporarily closed and as for getting permission to land at any of the helipads, well, that was a non-starter. Believe me, I tried. I even went as far as contacting Jonty Miller to see if I could borrow his private helicopter for the week but the lucky bastard's shacked up with some Parisian model in Monaco." He opened his mouth to say something further when, with a crash and a curse, a large man with a black, braided beard, stumbled down the small flight of steps leading to the lounge. The drink-laden tray he carried went flying.

"Can you get me…some water?" Summers mumbled.

"Of course." Torrence rose from his chair, stepped over an unfortunate sprawled on the floor and filled a plastic cup at a water fountain. He returned and set the drink on the table. "Here. Just sip it."

Summers took a much-needed drink, aware of the importance of not dehydrating. Was it just wishful thinking on his part or was the rocking beginning to subside? Through the windows, he could see glimpses of blue sky as opposed to the continuous, roiling grey which had pervaded since leaving, and the waves did seem to be getting smaller as the weather conditions improved.

The captain came on over the tannoy system, announcing that the worst of the storm was over and that for the remainder of the voyage the forecast looked fair. He hoped to be able to pick up a bit of speed and that the expected time of arrival at Tindholmur would remain as scheduled.

Over the next half an hour, bodies that had appeared lifeless began to stir.

"Ah, it reminds me of Spring," Torrence commented sarcastically as he watched some of the sufferers rise from where they had been lying and get into their chairs. "All these flowers now emerging; the long sleep of Winter finally over."

"More like the *Dawn of the Dead*," Summers quipped. "There's a good number here that would be perfect for zombies. I daresay they wouldn't need any make-up." Now that he was no longer feeling ill, he found himself capable of taking in his surroundings in greater detail. What had previously been a grey, sickness-induced miasma of tenebrous forms had now coalesced into a picture of normality. He approximated there to be thirty or so people—some he knew from past encounters, but a large number were complete strangers. Torrence he had known since his time at university.

"Funny you should say that, for apparently this Morgenstein chappie is all in favour of his undead. This dungeon he's built is supposedly rampant with them. I was told that one of the quests he's designed makes that gauntlet run we did last year in Cyprus look easy."

"I've still got the bloody scars from that. Look!" Summers unrolled his sleeve, exposing the bare flesh of his right arm from the elbow down. A pale, two inch long wound was plainly visible against his tanned skin. "I've got another, just as bad on my left thigh."

"Well, maybe this time you'll see some sense and go as a warrior—none of this wizard crap. Get yourself fully kitted out in some decent armour. Trust me. You can't always rely on a judge to be present and sometimes it pays to just batter the living hell out of your enemy."

* * * *

In the time between the captain announcing that they were approaching their destination and getting off the boat, Summers found himself reflecting on the circumstances that had brought him to this godforsaken place. It was a given that many 'normal' folk would think that his idea of fun went way beyond lunacy. He accepted this, well-aware that society—certainly the stinkingly rich, professional, educated circles in which he operated—had an uneasy outlook on grown men and women pretending to be spell-casters and monster-killers. He had been introduced to the world of live-action role playing or *larping* as it was commonly known whilst at Oxford, having lost interest in academia and punting. Initially it been a dare, proposed by one of his fellow Bullingdon Club Members and he had been utterly bemused by the whole experience. It had been then that he had met Torrence, the two quickly forming a firm friendship as they had dashed through the woods, attired in leather armour and hacking and slashing at bizarrely made-up strangers. There was a thrill to be had, not knowing when or from where an enemy would strike.

As a child, he had been brought up on the works of Tolkien, so it was no great leap of the imagination to embrace the fantastical element of this newly-found interest. The highly popular *Dungeons and Dragons* was undoubtedly another influence but to him it was a poor substitute to what he considered to be the real thing. After all, there was only a limited amount of entertainment to be had from sitting around a table with a group of spotty-faced nerds rolling dice, certainly when compared to putting oneself right into the heart of the action. There was no doubt that actuality surpassed virtuality.

Upon leaving university with a lower second degree in Economics, he had secured immediate employment in his father's law firm. Three years later, he had opted for a career change; managing various banking groups, principally in the private sector. He had then delved into the intricacies of the Stock Exchange, until finally entering big business as a financial analyst.

Making money was undeniably nice but as far as he was concerned it was but a means to an end. He had become ensnared by the live role-playing bug; becoming president of the Southern England division within a matter of months, his duties largely concerning organising events and arranging venues.

Like all clubs and societies, the membership varied considerably and there was no denying the fact that larping did attract the weird and the wonderful.

* * * *

Summers disembarked from the boat at the small stone jetty on the remote Faroe Island of Tindholmur, his clothes stained with dried vomit, one would have found it hard to believe that he was a multi-millionaire. Indeed, as he stumbled along the gangway, in the company of others who looked as equally sordid and dishevelled, an outside observer could well have thought that he was a refugee, an asylum-seeker or part of a group that had been rescued from some naval calamity. He was still dizzy from motion sickness.

Like a line of bedraggled rats having just escaped the proverbial sinking ship, the group of thirty-six live-action role players made their way through the dark, the fog and the heavy drizzle onto the crude quayside. Some coughed and spluttered. Many of them were sick, tired and disorientated after having endured the most gruelling of crossings for, contrary to the captain's announcement, the last three hours had been just as atrocious as the first two.

"This had better be worth it," Seamus Hayes grumbled. "Ten grand this has cost me."

Summers was paying little attention to his Irish friend, his eyes trying to pierce the gloom in order to get some idea of his surroundings. Aside from the foul weather, his main impression was that of something huge—a mountain, perhaps—dominating the small island. He had purposefully not done any prior research on the geography or topography of Tindholmur, not wanting to spoil the surprise that came with self-discovery.

"I paid twenty," Torrence said, his heavy rucksack on his back.

Hayes turned in surprise. "*Twenty?*"

"Yes, an extra ten for the dungeon package—*The Maze of Morgenstein*," Torrence replied. "It's rumoured to be the best, most immersive dungeon experience out there. No one's ever met him but there's no doubt he's a genius and he's spent a shit-load of money on its design and construction. What's more, I believe there's a handsome prize waiting for the first group who succeed in getting through it."

* * * *

The accommodation was basic; a million miles from the five-star luxury many of those present were used to. It comprised of three long cabin-like huts—one for the eleven women who had arrived and the remaining two for the men. Each guest was allocated a bunk and a cupboard for the storage of personal items.

The man who was showing Summers' group around was young, wiry, bespectacled and had a mop of black curly hair. He had introduced himself earlier as Frederick and en route to the huts he had told them that he was a Danish national as well as an experienced mountaineer.

"This place is like a prison camp," Hayes moaned as the group neared an outbuilding.

Summers had to agree. The interior was well lit by several large floodlights, enabling him to see the austere buildings and the barbed wire perimeter fence. He half-expected to see a machine-gun carrying sentry, cigarette in mouth and with a German Shepherd Dog on a leash step from the shadows. "Maybe it'll look better in the daylight."

"I don't suppose there's any room service?" Torrence inquired.

Frederick turned and mutely shook his head. "Here are the male toilets." He pushed open the door to what was obviously the lavatory and shower block.

"I'm starving. When do we eat?" Hayes asked.

"Breakfast is served at eight in the mess building, the one we went to first," Frederick answered. "Lunch is at two o'clock and an evening meal is arranged for between eight and ten. Hot drinks and snacks can be obtained from the vending machines."

An elderly man with a goatee and an ornate walking cane, whom Summers knew only as 'Nix the Necromancer' raised his hand. "I don't suppose there are any phones, are there? It's just that I'd agreed to give my wife a call, to let her know that I'd arrived safely."

Frederick shook his head. "No phones."

"What happens in the case of an emergency?" Summers asked. He could think of almost a dozen past instances when someone had been injured—a broken arm, a badly sprained wrist, even a severed finger. On one particularly unpleasant occasion a young woman he had been fighting alongside had been accidently blinded in the eye with one of the rubber-tipped arrows shot by a young boy guised as a goblin archer.

"We have fully trained medical staff on site." Frederick looked at his wristwatch. "Well, gentlemen. It's late and I daresay you've all had a tiring journey so may I suggest you make your way back to the cabin."

* * * *

Mercifully, the hangover which Summers had awoken with had dissipated to a mild and tolerable background headache by the time he left the dormitory with most of the others. The blinding sunlight and the bitterly cold, refreshing breeze were the first things to strike him upon stepping outside. The next was the looming sight of the mountainous, craggy, serrated peak that rose the best part of nine hundred feet into the clear blue sky, dominating everything else. He stopped and gazed in awe, craning his neck muscles as he traced the acutely-angled, grassy incline that reached up to the summit.

Hayes gawped at the sight, hands on hips. "Hope to God we don't have to go up there!"

Torrence lit one of his slender, exotic-smelling and extremely expensive cigarettes. "It doesn't look too bad a climb. I daresay it would only take a couple of hours."

Hayes laughed. "Well if we have to go up you can carry me."

As a group, they headed over to the canteen building.

It was busy and fairly noisy inside, most of the others already seated at two of the three long tables.

The aroma of good cooking hung in the air and Summers noted that the food was all laid out, buffet-style, at the approach to a small kitchen. Taking his plate, he joined the fast-moving and efficient queue, soon helping himself to a plentiful amount of bacon, scrambled egg, toast, devilled kidneys and mushrooms. After he had poured himself a large glass of tomato juice, he found somewhere to sit. He was famished and his stomach was empty. The fry-up was delicious; the best cooked breakfast he had eaten in a long time. If the other meals were even remotely like this then he could forgive the austere sleeping conditions.

"I'm going up for seconds," said Hayes after having devoured somewhere in the region of three and a half thousand calories of high-fat meat and dairy products. He returned a minute later, his plate piled high. He sat down. "Ah, just what the doctor ordered."

"Greedy bastard," Torrence commented dryly. He was by far more reserved when it came to food and drink; his breakfast having been but a half-bowl of muesli.

"I've paid for it, so I'm going to bloody well make sure I get my money's worth." Unashamedly, Hayes scooped up a rasher of bacon and forked it into his mouth.

Summers was just about to get up in order to get himself another tomato juice when there came a loud gonging sound.

Silence fell as though by magic.

All eyes turned as a concealed door at the far end of the hall opened and a bald-headed, Oriental-looking man in a long black robe which was decorated with purple dragons stepped forth, gong in hand. His left eye was covered by a black eyepatch adding to his overall weirdness. "Esteemed guests. Adventurers from realms far and far seeming, I am Zoog." He reached into a pocket of his robe and removed a small scroll which he began to read from. "My master, Morgenstein, greets you warmly and well to the island. Here you will find fantasies beyond your wildest imagination; creatures born of nightmare, treasures beyond worth and quests, fiendishly designed to challenge the wisest. Know too, that your actions are at all times watched by the All-Seeing, All-Powerful, Morgenstein, who, from the moment you stepped into his domain, has been observing you. Your lives…are his to control." There was a pause as the man put the scroll away. When he next spoke his tone was completely different. "Right, now that the theatrics are over with…let's get down to the practicalities on how we're going to do things. Beneath your chairs, you'll find a sealed envelope. Please take this out, open it and remove the piece of folded paper contained within. Whatever you do, make sure no one else sees it. On this, you will find information on your character's background; reasons for coming here, agenda, quest notes and all that kind of stuff I daresay many of you as experienced larpers are familiar with."

During the next minute or so, people put aside their cutlery and retrieved the sealed envelopes, opening them to discover what role they were expected to play whilst on the island.

Summers drew out his brief and read it to himself.

Greetings,

You are a human warrior, merciless and cold-hearted, from the bustling city of Lyadra who has come to the island in search of fortune and glory. Your quest is to be the first to find the Chalice of Circe. Only by completing this task can you gain the experience required to advance to the next level.

Remember, I will be watching.

M.

"I trust that everyone has had a chance to read through their individual instructions?" Zoog glanced from side to side.

With some effort, 'Nix the Necromancer' got to his feet. "This is all a bit…*unusual*."

"*Unusual?* In what way?" Zoog asked.

"Well, wherever I go I always play the same character as many here will testify. It's what I'm best suited to. Yet, according to what's on this sheet of paper, I've got to—"

"Don't say!" Zoog interrupted, with a wag of a finger. "Well, I'm sorry if you're finding these rules somewhat different to what you're accustomed to, but, believe me, this tried and tested system has been shown to bring out the best in true role-players. Yes, it undoubtedly calls on a greater level of creativity and adaptation but it is done to enhance the enjoyment of something which could otherwise become quite repetitive. A warrior today, a warrior tomorrow, a warrior the week after…sounds a bit boring doesn't it? There is a positive amount of satisfaction to be gained playing a role which deviates from what one is familiar and comfortable with. After all, the whole idea is to let one's imagination reign supreme."

"This is a load of bollocks!" A thick-set man with a white beard and a Welsh accent rose to his feet. "I don't care what you say or what's on this." Angrily, he waved the sheet of personal instructions he held in his hand. "I'm William Wyvern-Killer…a mighty knight from the forgotten city of Kar-Diff; always have been and always will be. So, if you think I've paid ten grand to come here and be a…" Putting on his spectacles, he read aloud from the note, "…'an elf wizard, whose greatest claim to fame is to be able to calm enemies with the soothing sound of your melodious voice and whose reason to come to the island is to find true love,' then you can think again!" In a fit of rage, he tore the page in half and threw it down on the table. "Bloody ridiculous! I mean, look at me for Christ's sake! I've come here to knock heads together not ponce about on the grass with flowers in my hair!"

Two other men got to their feet, voicing similar complaints. One of them making the extremely valid point that he, like the majority there, had brought his own personalised costume—one that was designed with a particular character in mind.

"I regret that those are the rules," Zoog replied. "The rules that must be adhered to."

The Welshman shook his head. "Well, you know what you can do with your rules, don't you?"

Zoog calmly crossed his arms. "No, tell me."

Summers did not know whether it was his overactive imagination or something else but he suddenly had the strange feeling that the Oriental-looking man *did* possess a hidden, mage-like power and that with a wave of his hand 'William Wyvern Killer' would either go up in a puff of smoke or be transformed into a toad.

The Welshman obviously felt the same for he proved unwilling to continue the argument. Muttering darkly to himself, he sat down.

There was an uncomfortable tension in the room, with many no doubt wondering just what they had got themselves into. After all, here they were, miles from anywhere, devoid of any means to reach the outside world and things had just turned more than a little awkward.

Zoog clapped his hands. "Now, you will also notice a small star on the top right corner of your page, the colour of which will determine which group you will join, thus determining who will be your fellow adventurers." He glanced at the large circular clock on the wall. "At nine o'clock could those with a red star make their way outside. Those with a blue star, twenty past nine. Green, twenty to ten. Yellow, ten o'clock. White, twenty past ten. Orange, twenty to eleven and finally, those with a black star, eleven o'clock." He looked around, questioningly. "Has everyone got that?"

Summers had been allocated with a black star, so he realised he would be one of those remaining when the rest had gone. In some way, he saw this as an advantage for it meant that he could have more to eat if he so chose but also, and more importantly, it would enable him to make a mental note of who was in which group. It was information that could prove of use in fulfilling the quest he had been assigned.

* * * *

Over the course of the next two hours or so, Summers drank coffee and watched observantly as those members in the various groups left the building at their appropriate times. As the minutes ticked away and the numbers gradually thinned, he was somewhat dismayed to note that neither Torrence nor Hayes were going to be part of his team, both having left simultaneously as players belonging to the white-star group.

Those with orange stars left the mess hall.

Summers did not recognise any of those remaining. There were three men and one woman. Aware that he was to adopt the persona of a human warrior and that a well-balanced party would require at least one spellcaster and a rogue, he found himself pre-guessing just who was going to be what. A nervous sense of apprehension crept into him—it was something he had experienced many times before, particularly when he was required to sit and wait.

Throughout the segregation, Zoog had remained mostly silent.

At eleven o'clock, the black star group got to their feet and headed for the exit.

Summers had expected there to be an adjudicator but aside from the four others there was no one to be seen.

"Hmm. Now what do we do?" The woman—a frumpy, bespectacled individual with dyed purple hair and a bad case of acne, was nonplussed. Her bare, muscular arms were covered in strange, Celtic-themed tattooes.

"Christ knows, but we're being watched." Summers pointed to a surveillance camera mounted high up on the side of the mess hall. "Anyway, the name's Chris."

"Frankie." The purple-haired woman nodded.

"I'm Sam." A tall, dark-haired man with grey sideburns and a week's growth of stubble raised his right hand by way of introduction. "Sam McGee. Pleased to meet you all." He spoke with an American accent.

"Roy Bridger," an elderly, bespectacled man with a short iron-grey beard who was dressed in a tweed jacket announced.

"And who are you, my friend?" McGee asked the hairy, warty-faced man who had remained stand-offish as though unwilling to engage with the others.

"K'teshra," the man snarled as he jabbed his thumb to his puffed-out chest. "Half-orc. Warrior. Slayer of the Barrow Wyrms." He raised a clenched fist. "I WILL KILL ALL WHO OPPOSE ME!"

Summers took a step back, his ears ringing from the unexpected bellow. It was just his luck to get someone who was unhinged in his group—either that or the guy had decided to get into character from the word go. He could only hope it was the latter.

"Good to have you on *our* side," said McGee.

"You lot!"

They all turned upon hearing the shout. Rushing towards them, bloody sword in hand, the suit of chain mail he wore clinking, came a man. He was tall and well-built with a short black beard that was flecked through with grey. His eyes were pale blue and piercing

"We must get out of here! This place will soon be overrun with them. Quickly, come with me."

As a group they followed at a fast march.

The stranger led them around the far side of the mess hall towards a gate in the perimeter fence.

Summers was surprised that he could not see any of the teams that had left earlier, reasoning that the groups had been purposefully dispersed so that each could be instructed in their particular goals. Passing the huge wooden gate, he saw that a broad swathe of lush green headland extended for several hundred yards before it sloped down to the sea. Over to his left, the imposing peak loomed tall and menacing. This had to be one of the most barren and inhospitable places he had ever visited.

"This way!" For a middle-aged man in a suit of armour, the stranger moved reasonably fast as he headed for the cliff edge. He was obviously a skilled actor and keen to play his role for he kept turning to glance over his shoulder as though fearful of something. Reaching the precipitous drop, he raised his free hand, signalling to the others to stop. "Hurry! There's a safe way down. I'll explain everything when we're safe." Scrambling over a few rocks, the biting wind now gusting straight off the sea and directly towards him and his small group, he started down a flight of worn stone steps that gave access to the beach.

Summers gave a wry smile, appreciating the effort the man was putting into his role-playing even though he considered it a bit hammy. He was the last of the group to begin the descent and from his raised vantage point, he could see that the coastline stretched for some half a mile before it disappeared around the southern edge of the island. The steps which had been cut into the cliff-face were hazardous and there was no protective rail so it was with a great deal of caution that he made his way down.

The armoured man waited for them all to gather. Without a word spoken, he then set off once more, striding out across the rugged beach.

"How much further?" Bridger shouted. "It's just that my legs aren't too good."

"Not far!" Sword held firmly, the man turned and pointed to a concealed door; painted grey and camouflaged against the cliff wall. Leading his group across the final fifty yards or so of beach, he went up to it and pulled it open. "Everyone inside! Quick, before we're seen!"

Lowering his head slightly, Summers entered a small cave-like room. At first view, he reckoned it was a natural hollow, no doubt scoured out of the cliff-face by the erosive powers of the elements but the more he saw made him think that it had been artificially created. In the centre was a table, around which were six wooden stools. Several crates and old-fashioned trunks lay in a hewn-out niche.

The door slammed shut and three stout metal bolts were drawn.

"I didn't think he would but he has. He…he's done it! He's actually done it!" Whether it was due to the fact that they had reached the relative safety of the cave, the chain mail clad man's whole persona seemed to have changed. "He's truly lost it." His eyes were glazed and unseeing. With a stumble, he fell against the table, straightened unsteadily and then sat down, grasping his head in his hands.

The five larpers exchanged bemused glances.

"Sorry, what are you on about?" Bridger asked.

"And who are you?" Summers inquired.

The man slumped at the table looked up. "My name's…" He paused, clearly contemplating the wisdom in indulging that information. "You can call me…Xanathos." He took a deep breath. "The others are dead…or as good as."

Either Xanathos was an extremely good actor or he was telling the truth—for something in the manner in which he made this claim made Summers uneasy. "What…others?"

"Why, those poor bastards who came with you to the island."

"Sorry, I don't understand." McGee said. "Just what's going on here?"

"He's just playing his character," Frankie answered rationally. From the tone of her voice it was obvious that she, at least, was of the opinion that this was all just part of the adventure.

"I wish that were the case." Xanathos shook his head.

"So…what…what's this all about?" Summers stammered, his voice weak. His mind was a raging cauldron of whirling emotions and a sick knot of fear and anxiety had developed in his gut. Surely this was all just words—a falsehood—created to set the mood of the role-playing experience. That had to be it. He relaxed a little at the thought that no doubt those in the other groups were in all likelihood being told a similar story. Perhaps it was done in order to instil a degree of uncertainty and concern in order to heighten the whole experience.

"In a word…*madness*." Xanathos slid his sword across the table towards where K'teshra stood. "It may be best that you take this and stand guard at the door while I tell you what's really happening here on this accursed island."

"Look, before you go any further—is this 'game-talk' or is this real?" Bridger asked.

"This is real, although how I wish to God it wasn't." Xanathos seemed to have relaxed a little now that he had positioned someone at the cave entrance. "Max Morgenstein, the designer of this hell-hole is a psychopath. Yes, he's a multi-millionaire and a genius but he's mad, insane; crazy beyond belief. For over ten years he's spent God knows how much burrowing into and below Tindholmur; creating a real-life dungeon which he's filled with deadly traps and…man-made monsters. You five are the fortunate ones in that unlike the others who are either dead or have been 'changed' through the use of a mind-altering nerve gas, you, at least, have the opportunity to face his lethal maze through which none, to date, have managed to—"

"I've had enough of this!" McGee got to his feet. "I've paid good money to come here but honestly this is taking things a bit too far. I've been to live-role playing events all over the world and I've never know anything like this before. I'll be the first to agree it's an interesting set-up but…in my mind, it's just plain wrong."

"You're taking it all too seriously." Frankie looked at her fellow larpers. "I mean, come on. Let's put things into some kind of perspective here, shall we? I daresay in three hours or so, when we're all sat down at lunch, we'll be joking about how we spent the morning worrying about something as stupid as this. After all, let's face it, if this Morgenstein had decided to bump off thirty or so of us there's a lot of people knew I was coming here and remote as it may be it wouldn't take that long for the police to find out what has *supposedly* happened."

"Which is why the captain of the boat you all arrived on late yesterday evening had been ordered to send out a distress signal, stating that your ship had ran into difficulties and was sinking some two hundred miles south-east of here." Xanathos scratched at his growth of beard. "So, you see, as far as anyone knows, you're all already dead."

There was a certain surrealness to all that had transpired over the past half an hour or so that Summers was finding hard to come to terms with. He was unwilling to accept that there was any kind of truth behind what had been said; his mind baulking at the idea that his two friends—Torrence and Hayes—not to mention the others he had been having breakfast with that very morning, had fallen victim to some maniac. It was absolute lunacy—it had to be.

"This is all bollocks." Frankie gave a disparaging shake of her head. "A clever, unsettling back story concocted to provide something a little extra to our adventure. If any of you want to believe it, then fine, that's how it's supposed to be. Personally, I'd rather just get what I've paid for and explore this dungeon."

"But what if it's true?" Bridger asked nervously. He looked as though he was on the verge of tears. "As far as I know no one has ever clapped eyes on this Morgenstein character. He could be mad enough to do something like this."

"So what are we going to do about it?" Summers asked. He was trying his utmost to keep his emotions under control, to accept this situation in the manner that Frankie was—to hope that it was all just a big hoax generated in order to enhance the interactive experience.

"I say we go back and find out just what the hell's going on. You lot can do what you want but that's what I'm doing." McGee made his way to the door by which they had entered.

Like some nightclub bouncer, K'teshra stood rock-steady, barring the way.

"Can I get out?" McGee asked politely.

K'teshra growled menacingly.

Summers gulped nervously, silently willing the American to back down and return to his seat. His initial impression that the individual who had been chosen to play a half-orc warrior was unhinged now proving true. Either that or he was somehow involved in this unfolding and disturbing drama. At the back of his mind, he had a terrible image of the hirsute, biker-type suddenly making a swing with the sword he had been armed with, chopping McGee down.

"Will you *please* step aside?" McGee said.

"If you go out, you die," K'teshra snarled. "Shut up and listen!"

At first Summers could not hear a thing aside from the odd little fidgeting of those around him. Several seconds passed, and then there came a faint wailing from outside, followed by the troubling shouts of angry voices. Having spent many weekends in a top hotel in Glasgow city centre, it was a noise he knew well—and it heralded danger.

McGee spun round to look at Xanathos. "What the hell's that?"

Xanathos got to his feet. "Your cue to get kitted up and act the roles you've been assigned to act. That's assuming you want to get out of here in one piece. Now do it and do it fast!"

This was only the second time Summers had ever donned a suit of chain mail and unlike that former occasion, he heeded the advice given and put on a heavy cloth jerkin beforehand so that it would cushion any blows and reduce chafing. Like the others, he dressed hastily, unnerved by the approaching cries coming from outside. Under a cloak, he found a kite-shaped shield which had been embossed with the design of a rearing black dragon and a matching surcoat.

"Don't forget these." Xanathos hefted a bulging sack on to the table, opening it up to reveal a collection of weapons—three swords, a mace, a dagger, a battle axe, two spiked clubs and a slender, six-foot long quarter staff. "You're going to need them."

Frankie was the first to them. "Jesus! These are real!" Tentatively, she picked up the double-bladed axe.

Summers stared, open-mouthed.

"Of course they are? What were you expecting—plastic ones?" Xanathos gestured for K'teshra to step aside so that he could put his ear to the door. A moment later, he turned round. "I'd hurry it up if I were you. They're getting nearer."

"Surely to Christ we're not going to fight each other with these?" Bridger had obviously been assigned the role of party wizard for he had clothed himself in an ankle-length silvery grey robe and he had a crumpled conical hat of the same colour on his head. "And what spells have I got to cast?"

"You still don't get it, do you?" Xanathos said. "You're now in a life or death situation. It's a case of kill or be killed."

That there was something really weird going on Summers had no doubt but he was undecided over just what was truth and what was lie. However, given the circumstances, the only thing he could think of was to permit this unfolding scenario to play itself out. Having reached that conclusion, he went over to the table and calmly picked up one of the swords. He would play the part of a warrior, merciless and cold-hearted, from the bustling city of Lyadra and woe betide anyone who got in his way.

Without warning, there came a resounding thump on the door.

Bridger screamed.

"Are we going to have to fight our way out?" Summers asked grimly. Although he could not see whatever was outside, from the hideous, gargling screams, he would bet good money for it to be a small army of zombies. Requiring minimal make-up, along with orcs and goblins, the flesh-eating undead were a common staple of the many larping events he had been to.

"No! From the sounds of it there are too many of them. Besides, there's another way." Xanathos went to the rear of the cave and began searching for something. A moment later, he pulled a camouflaged panel aside, revealing a darkened opening beyond.

Grasping her battle axe and clad in a mismatched array of plate mail and studded leather armour, Frankie stomped over, a horned helmet on her head. "Ah, the old secret door escape route. Fortune shines on us. Mayhaps this leads to the dungeon and enough gold to buy us passage off this island of dread."

More frantic screams came from outside, accompanying the savage battering on the door.

Summers turned, half-expecting to see a ravenous tide of scabrous, green-faced folk to come pouring inside, arms outstretched. A battle would then ensue, pitching his small party against the 'animated corpses'. Hopefully an adjudicator—maybe Xanathos—would take charge, gauging the outcome of the skirmish. However, the use of real weapons was of deep concern. Someone could get seriously injured.

Having outfitted himself in a steel breastplate, K'teshra patted his spiked club, ready and more than willing to beat the living daylights out of anything that he considered a danger.

"Quick! Follow me!" Xanathos disappeared into the hidden passage.

McGee was only half-dressed. Frantically, he pulled on a pair of tight-fitting leggings and then fastened a cloak around his neck. Of all of them he was without doubt the least convinced that this was but a game.

Stepping back from the door, Summers retreated to the tunnel mouth into which Frankie, Bridger and K'teshra had already gone.

A strong stink of dankness wafted from the subterranean darkness.

The hammering on the door was increasing and whilst Summers thought it would hold, providing those outside did not start hacking at it with axes, he knew that it was imperative that they got going.

Sheathing his sword, he grabbed McGee and pulled him back into the secret passage.

"Will you two hurry it up!?" Frankie's plea echoed along the tunnel.

"Where does this go?" Summers asked as he caught up with the others. Faint illumination came from what looked like a lantern ensconced into the wall some fifteen yards further along the corridor.

"It leads to Morgenstein's labyrinth," Xanathos answered. "Indeed, this is part of it—a veritable warren of interconnecting passageways and hidden chambers."

"I take it you know how to get through?" Bridger asked concernedly.

Xanathos nodded. "Some of it. Although it won't be easy. It was designed to be a deathtrap."

* * * *

It was overwhelmingly obvious to Summers that this entire underground complex must have cost millions, indeed tens of millions of pounds to create. The sheer scale and level of detail bordered on the unbelievable and if it was not for the underlying potential menace which hounded his every step, he would have easily succumbed to the full fantastical ambience that the place instilled. It was the archetypal dungeon—the kind of setting which in his imagination, he had envisaged himself in a thousand times. In all of his larping experience he had never been in anything as realistic as this.

They entered a vaulted chamber that was approximately the same size as the mess hall. In the opposite wall were three wooden doors, banded with metal.

"This place is amazing!" Frankie said, doing a full circle and gazing up at the ceiling.

"It's certainly impressive," Summers agreed. Even in the shadowy lantern light, he could make out the smaller, finer touches which had been added in order to increase the authenticity of the place; the scattered bones, the occasional broken weapon, the odd splash of blood and damp footprint—features designed to enhance the believability and authenticity of Morgenstein's Maze. Whether due to the nuances of the architecture or the odour of dampness and decay which permeated the air, the subterranean vault possessed a certain timeless antiquity, giving it the appearance of great age despite the fact that it had, certainly to his knowledge, been built within the last ten years or so.

"I've never seen anything like this before," Bridger commented.

"Come on! We don't have time to waste!" Xanathos was standing by the three doors. With a tug, he pulled open the one nearest to him.

In a moment of sheer horror that took Summers by complete surprise, there came a ghastly howl. In the same instant, he saw a huge hairy arm shoot out of the darkness, claw extended. It grabbed hold of Xanathos and hauled him inside. The door was then slammed shut.

"Jesus Christ!" McGee shouted.

"That was a troll! I saw it!" Battle axe gripped tightly, Frankie moved towards the door. She turned and glanced at the others. "Well come on you cowardly bastards! We have to save him."

Bridger gulped nervously. "I…I'm not so sure about this."

Summers too was unsure about the wisdom of re-opening that door, just as he was unsure about this whole experience. From the outset it had been completely different to the far more organised and typical larping adventures he had been involved with. This was disturbing and potentially dangerous whereas those others had been enjoyable and at times downright hilarious. What fun there was to be had here had yet to materialise.

"Hmm. Troll, nasty. I think our friend already dead." K'teshra gave a low, displeased growl. "Maybe we should try another door?"

"Am I the only sane one here?" McGee looked around questioningly. "Do you lot think this is just a game?"

"Of course it's only a bloody game!" Frankie shouted. "And right now, we've got a friend to rescue." With that, she rushed over to the door and pulled hard on the iron ring handle.

The door would not budge.

Gritting her teeth, Frankie pulled harder. "Half-orc! Get over here and give us a hand with this, will you?"

"I take no orders from the likes of you." K'teshra stood his ground. "We must choose another way."

Even at this early stage in the fantasy role-playing, Summers could tell that these two were experienced in enacting whatever roles they had been assigned. Although Frankie had not, as yet, disclosed the nature of the character she had been assigned, it seemed fairly obvious to him that she was a dwarven battle-maiden; hardy, forthright and always up for a fight.

Frankie put an ear to the door.

"Anything?" Summers asked.

With a shake of her head, Frankie stepped back. "This door won't yield and now we've lost our party leader. Getting through this maze isn't going to be easy…or pleasant, but if we use our wits and stick together we may yet see daylight once again."

"Bonkers! Absolute raving bonkers!" McGee was in despair. He looked forlornly at Summers. "You…you look like you've got some sense. What's your take on all of this?"

"If you're asking me whether or not I think that this Dungeon Master or whatever he is has murdered everyone who came with us, then…no," Summers replied. "I'll freely admit that our missing friend was pretty convincing and it's the kind of thing that makes you stop and think, but when you look at it with a rational head you see that it's just too far-fetched. Besides what's he got to gain?"

"Why, money of course! And lots of it." Something caught McGee's eye and he bent to pick up a long, discoloured limb bone. "And what do you make of this? This is…human."

"Bollocks!" Frankie said, stepping close to have a look. "It's just some kind of plastic."

McGee held the femur out, exhibiting it for them to see. "I've got a Masters Degree in human biology so I should know." He spotted some more bones strewn in a corner. "And there's a human skull and part of a ribcage."

"Could be he's got a partnership with the local grave-robber," Summers quipped. "Maybe he gets these things on the cheap. Anyway, I don't see how—"

"*Quiet!* I hear voices." K'teshra moved to the opening through which they had entered.

Straining his senses, Summers could now pick out the faint cries which emanated from far behind them. There was little doubt it was the ravening horde that had been outside. Somehow they had forced the door open and were now advancing towards them. Even though he tried to force himself to believe that this was nothing but a well pre-planned game, the dread and the horror was enough to get his pulse racing.

"Shit!" Bridger cried. "Now what do we do?"

"Bugger this! I say we stand and fight." K'teshra patted his spiked club. "Let us return these dogs to the graves they've crawled from."

"You're all mad!" McGee was trembling with fear. "Don't any of you understand? They're going to kill us! We have to get out of here!"

At the very limit of his vision, at the far end of the tunnel, Summers could discern the first of the shambling shapes. He found himself doubting his own reasoning; his mind unwelcomingly entertaining that slim possibility that McGee was right—that Morgenstein had somehow transformed the others into hideous, mindless monsters. The fact that they had been armed with genuine weapons and that there was no adjudicator present was also troubling. A sudden noise behind him made him spin round whereupon he saw Frankie stood at the threshold of the middle door.

The screams in the darkness were getting louder.

"Come on! Hurry it up!" Frankie shouted.

Summers rushed over. "We don't even know where this goes."

"Well, what do you want to do?" Frankie asked, her tone belligerent. "We either risk this passage, we try the other door or we probably all die…that is in the game, of course; torn to pieces and devoured by those zombies."

With a hand gesture, Summers acquiesced. "Then lead on."

"Right. Follow me…and that includes you half-orc." Clearly relishing being in charge, now that Xanathos had gone, Frankie turned and stomped hurriedly along the passage, her ragtag party close on her heels.

* * * *

The wails had died down by the time the passage they were heading along came to an end at a flight of steps leading up. Here they paused.

"Methinks this dungeon extends over several levels." Stroking her chin as though it were a pretend beard, Frankie stared up into the darkness. "It's not dwarven built that's for sure. You only have to look at the quality of the stonework to know that."

Incapable of making any sense in the situation, McGee shook his head in annoyance.

"Friend, does something trouble you?" Frankie asked gruffly.

"I just want to get out of here," McGee replied.

"Don't we all," Summers said. "But therein lies the problem."

"Like you, I want nothing more than to get out of here and get off this island." Bridger leant wearily against a wall. "This isn't what I bargained for when I sent off my application to come here. However, in case you haven't noticed, we're trapped down here. The only way is onward."

McGee tore off his cloak and threw it to the ground. "This is pissing me off, big time. I hate being underground. I hate not knowing what's going on and I sure as hell hate this Morgenstein. This is torture, psychological torture. Pure and simple."

"Don't you think you're exaggerating things a bit?" Summers asked.

"*Exaggerating things?*" McGee put his hands on his hips. "Sorry, am I hearing right? What was it that Xanathos guy told us? That Morgenstein has gone nuts and killed—"

"It's just a game!" Frankie interrupted. "However, I hope you realise you're spoiling it for everybody else. This constant worrying and whining. Why don't you just do as the rest of us are, and get into character? Try it. It's fun."

McGee was temporarily at a loss for words. Reluctantly, he stooped down and retrieved his cloak.

"The air smells fresher up there," K'teshra said, a foot on the lowest step.

"Then let's go!" Demonstrating her ebullience and plucky determination, Frankie bounded up the steps, her battle axe swinging in her hand.

Higher and higher the stairway wound.

In places, shafts of grey daylight shone through crevices in the rocky wall and Summers realised that they were progressing up the interior of the huge mountain that rose from Tindholmur. It truly was a remarkable feat of engineering.

Eventually the stairway ended at an arched opening.

After walking down the passage beyond, they came to another chamber. At one end, a cracked flight of stone steps led up into the ruined darkness, the way blocked by the collapsed ceiling. Smashed pillars and huge piles of detritus formed small mountains of rubble. Niches and alcoves around the walls housed many age-worn statues, giving the adventurers the unnerving sense that they were being watched from the shadows.

In the centre Frankie and K'teshra were mulling over which way to go.

Summers could see three doors; two directly opposite and one in the right wall. The left wall was adorned with an amazing mural which depicted a gang of rampaging ogres attacking a settlement of cowering people. In another scene, a monstrous indigo octopus grappled and constricted numerous hapless underwater beings. In one corner, a shadowy figure was shown sitting astride a flaming dragon, swooping down from the nightmare skies to bring death and destruction to those below.

Frankie turned on hearing Summers approach. "Any suggestions?"

"I say we go that way." K'teshra pointed to the solitary door on the right.

"That's as good as any, I guess," Summers replied wearily. He went over to the huge wall painting in order to examine it better. Even though the lighting was poor, he could see that the work of art was of outstanding quality, the painting covering the entire wall of the chamber from floor to ceiling. Stepping closer, he walked to one side, suitably impressed by the dynamic manner in which many of the scenes had been worked. Although he had no idea of the identity of the unknown artist responsible for this masterpiece there was little doubt in his mind concerning the exceptional talents that individual possessed.

Panting like a sick dog and clutching at his chest, McGee stumbled up the stairs. Having now completed the ascent he went to the nearest wall and slumped down absolutely exhausted. Within moments, he was muttering darkly to himself.

Finally, Bridger appeared. If anything, he looked even more physically drained that McGee.

"Wizard!" Frankie called out. "Do you see anything in this painting which may give us a clue as to which route to take?"

"For pity's sake, let him be," Summers said. He had failed to notice anything within the mural which might prove helpful and despite knowing from past larping experience the thing to do was to call out what he was intending so that an adjudicator could decide on the outcome of said action, he remained silent. With no accompanying referees it was hard to determine what rules, if any, were in place pertaining to this dungeon.

"Surely you'd agree it's vital that we go the right way?" Frankie retorted. "Or maybe you'd rather just blunder into a room full of monsters or some killer trap?"

"To tell you the truth, right now I don't give a—" Summers was interrupted by a sudden loud crash. Turning round, he was horrified to see that one of the two side-by-side doors had fallen forward, on top of which lay a man's body.

"Christ!" Bridger exclaimed, raising a hand to his mouth in shock.

"Holy shit!" cried McGee, getting to his feet.

Summers walked over, his heart sinking for there was no motion—no twitching or signs of breathing—signifying that the man was quite dead. As he neared, he could see that the corpse was punctured in several places, fresh blood pooling beneath it. "What the hell is this!?" He crouched down, and tried in vain to detect a pulse, averting his gaze from the blood-spattered face which was contorted into a ghastly rictus.

K'teshra and Frankie looked on in stunned silence.

"Is he dead?" Bridger asked.

"As a dodo," Summers answered.

"He…was sat…sat my ta-table," Bridger stammered. "He asked me…to pass the bu-butter."

"There are spikes under this door," said Frankie. "It looks like a two-way door trap. Look! You can see where it's counterbalanced at the base. There!" She pointed. "You can see the central pivot."

"She's right," McGee confirmed. He noticed a small box-like compartment inset into the wall near the door jamb. "I'm no expert but this looks like some sort of timer mechanism. Poor bastard must've been stood by the door when it went off, causing the spikes to shoot out and for it to fall on him. He wouldn't have stood a chance." He turned to the others in the group. "Maybe now you believe when I say we're in the lair of a madman."

"It…could have been a tragic accident," Summers suggested, aware of the lameness of his own argument.

"*Tragic accident!* What are you on about?" McGee replied. "The poor bastard's been pinned to this door! Not only that, but that could very easily have been one of us."

"We need to get out of here," said Frankie. "If this was an unfortunate accident then we need to inform someone."

"And if not?" Bridger asked.

"Morgenstein dies." K'teshra stepped forward. "For this man was my brother."

Having now encountered one of the lethal contraptions this maze had been furnished with, the group proceeded with a heightened degree of caution. Doors were approached tentatively, greater attention was given to where they stood and nothing was touched unnecessarily. At one point Frankie, who led the way, had called an abrupt halt, fearing that she could smell gas and it was only after K'teshra confessed to a bout of flatulence that the all clear was given and the group resumed their search for the exit.

The passage they were going along was dark and dismal. Several darkened openings on either side gave access to further side passages.

Fake, though highly realistic, spider web hung from the low ceiling.

Summers found it hard to accept the severity of the situation he now found himself in. The thoughts that were constantly turning over in his mind had become as disagreeable as a bad meal. So many things refused to make sense, such as the latest revelation that the deceased they had discovered was related to K'teshra. It amazed him that aside from a suggestion of vengeance, the bereaved had shown little remorse. It was as though he was still playing his character.

"You know we've all failed the first test of every competent adventurer," Bridger said.

"What's that?" Summers asked.

"We should have started a map," Bridger answered. "As it is, we could be going round in circles. Indeed, some of this is beginning to look highly familiar."

Frankie turned. "My biggest fear at the moment is what happens if the lights go out. Then we'll really be in the shit!" She had hardly finished speaking when, as though bang on cue, the lights did go out, plunging them into utter darkness.

Like a steel gauntlet grasping his heart, instant fear struck Summers, freezing him to the core. A terrifying babble of sounds erupted all around him; cries, shouts, whimpers and the noisy grating of stone on stone. One of the others bumped into him, knocking him to one side. He reached out with a hand to support himself but the wall which he had seen only moments before had gone and he found himself stumbling forward through a mysterious gap and falling on to a hard stone floor. He landed sorely on his right knee, his sword falling from his hand and clattering nearby.

"*Morgenstein!* You bastard!"

Summers heard McGee's yell. There then came a maniacal laugh from somewhere nearby. More shouts. A scream and then the grinding noise he had heard before.

Silence.

Getting to his feet, Summers reached out blindly with his free hand, feeling nothing. "Is anybody there?" When his call went unanswered, he slowly and cautiously edged his way forward. From far-off or heavily muffled, he could not tell which, he heard another shout— or was it a scream? "Jesus Christ," he muttered to himself as he took another couple of tentative steps. At any moment he could fall into a pit or trigger some deadly device that could kill him outright. His heart was beating fast and a cold sweat broke out on his forehead. He stepped on his sword and bent down to retrieve it. Then he saw a faint sliver of yellow light from beneath what he assumed was a door over to his left. Tentatively, he made his way towards it.

There came a loud squeak. It was followed by others.

Summers jumped as he felt something brush against his left leg. It had to be a rat, and a large one at that. From the growing sound, there had to be a lot of them—a veritable swarm. Now spurred into throwing all caution to the wind, he made a rush for the gleam of light. It was a door. He found the handle and pulled it open to reveal a small room, less than ten foot square.

Half a dozen sleek black rats scurried inside.

Summers slammed the door shut behind him in order to keep out the seething mass of rodents that had undoubtedly been set loose by the evil genius behind this place of madness. They looked harmless enough although he knew how much different things would have been had he remained trapped in the darkness of that other room with hundreds of them. That would have been the stuff of nightmares. Still, his current situation could have been better for there did not appear to be any visible exits. As to where the rest of his group were that was anyone's guess. Given the nature of this warren under the mountain and its fiendish creator it could be that they were now dead.

"Ah, the warrior from Lyadra! How goes your search for the Chalice of Circe?"

Summers looked around in surprise, trying to pinpoint the source of that unearthly, disembodied voice. He waited, not knowing how to react—unsure as to whether or not he should initiate some kind of dialogue. The last thing he wanted to do right now was to give this Morgenstein the perverse satisfaction that he was completely at his mercy.

Without warning a section of wall nearby swung forward.

Raising his shield in order to protect himself from anything that might emerge from the space beyond, Summers was relieved to see K'teshra and Bridger. At least he would not have to face the perils of this nightmare labyrinth on his own.

"That was a bit hairy," Bridger commented.

K'teshra nodded mutely.

"The other two?" Summers asked.

"I don't know what happened to them when the lights went out," said Bridger. "We were both just behind you."

"Well, we'll have to go the way you came because this room behind us is heaving with rats." Summers kicked aside one of the creatures as it came close.

Bridger shook his head. "But that's a dead end. The wall's sealed us in. We were lucky to find this secret tunnel."

"Maybe there's another way out of this room," growled K'teshra. Without waiting for a reply to his suggestion, he began searching the stonework for any anomalies.

Summers and Bridger shared a resigned look and then they too set about looking for another way out.

After five minutes they had found nothing.

"This is not good!" Summers proclaimed in desperation. The thought that he was now trapped deep within a mountain, on a remote island miles from civilisation and in the company of two complete strangers—one of whom could have just escaped from a nuthouse—was enough to fill anyone with dread.

"It would appear that our only remaining option is to chance the rats," Bridger said. "Maybe, if we can lure some into this room and then— " He was interrupted by a sudden grating noise which was followed by a curse.

The three of them turned, surprised to see Frankie, sodden and covered in filth, haul herself from an opening in the ground. With a loud cough, she got to her feet.

"What the hell happened to you?" Summers asked.

"Bastard pit opened up right under my feet. I fell into a load of shit." Frankie wiped away a splatter of what looked like sewage from her forehead. "I thought I was going to drown in it."

"Is there a way out down there?" Bridger asked, pointing to the black square in the floor.

"There may be, but I should warn you, it isn't pleasant," Frankie replied.

"McGee?" Summers asked.

"I thought he was with you," Frankie answered. "Certainly wasn't with me."

"So where the hell's he got to?" Bridger asked concernedly.

Summers sighed audibly. "When I get out of here there's—"

"What makes you think you're *going* to get out of here?" K'teshra interrupted. Without waiting for a reply, he strode over to the opening in the floor.

Unsure as to whether the 'half-orc' had asked a pertinent question or had made a threat, Summers turned to Bridger, noting the troubled look that was mirrored on the elderly man's face.

"Well, if we've got to go back that way, I'd sooner we got it over with." Her boots squelching with mud and slime, Frankie walked over and joined K'teshra. She then got down on her knees and cautiously lowered herself backwards down the pit.

* * * *

How long they had been going, none could guess. In this stinking, sunless world of dank stone and ooze it was all too easy for the imagination to run wild; each new shadow or darkened opening a nightmare in waiting. They halted at a small chamber from which three other tunnels radiated.

The filthy water was knee-deep.

"To think I've paid over ten thousand pounds to wade through a sewer," Bridger commented glumly.

"It's beyond a bloody joke!" Summers replied. "This place stinks and we don't know where we're going." The only positive he could take from their predicament was the fact that, as in the corridors above, lanterns had been set into the walls, providing them with some illumination.

"I'd have thought you two would be experienced dungeoneers," Frankie commented over her shoulder.

"Yeah, but come on," Summers argued. "I've never had to do this kind of thing before. Most of the larping events I've been to in the past have been outdoors; places you don't have to escape from. Even on the odd occasion where there's been a ruin or a castle to explore, it's been nothing like this."

"You mean dangerous?" K'teshra said.

"Exactly," Summers answered sharply.

"Personally, I like the thrill; the element of realism. After all, is this not what it should be all about?" Frankie asked. "Life on the edge; our mettle, wits and cold steel pitted against the evil overlord. I know I might not make everyone happy, but I'll keep us alive."

Summers could scarcely believe what he was hearing. "Surely to Christ you still don't think this is a game? A man's been killed for God's sake and one of our group's missing!"

"Adds to the excitement, doesn't it?" Frankie replied matter of factly. She stepped back from the wall she had been leaning against. "Well, if we're going to get out of here I suggest we get moving."

"Okay, which way?" Summers asked brusquely.

Frankie made her way to the opening on their right. "Unless I'm imaging things, I'd say the light looks a bit brighter down this passage. Could be that it opens out into a larger area."

"Then that's the way we go." Without waiting for an agreement, K'teshra snatched up his spiked club and waded over to the exit in question. The next moment he was gone, disappearing into the shadowy darkness.

Frankie went next.

With a shake of his head and a perplexed, resigned look at Bridger, Summers followed. The sword in his hand offered him some sense of reassurance but he very much doubted whether he would be able to use the blade in a real life or death situation. It was one thing hitting strangers with rubber, plastic or hardened foam weapons but what he held, gripped in a tight grasp, was designed to kill or at the very least, inflict serious damage.

A thick stench from something unpleasant hung in the foul air, catching at the backs of their throats as they went along the long tunnel. Eventually it opened out into a large chamber.

Strange, phosphorescent moss provided a weird, purple-green illumination.

"By all the gods!" Frankie called out.

Eyes widening in awe, Summers thought for a moment that he really had stepped from the mundane, normal, sane world he knew into the mythical, fantastical realm of sword and sorcery for the space before him was gargantuan in scale—a cavernous vault, its peripheries shrouded in shadow. A preponderance of stalagmites sprouted from the roughly hewn ground and he could see an arched ruin, raised on a stepped dais. There were also huge, grotesque, misshapen, toadstool-like fungi, which, although he doubted were real, looked highly authentic.

"Just look at this place!" Bridger exclaimed in amazement.

As a group, the four of them slowly advanced towards the strange edifice. Cracked statues leered at them from the shadows, their faces seemingly frozen in anger at this trespass. Some were twisted and fractured, little more than shattered heaps of half-buried statuary. Others were huge and towering, giant shapes laden with malice; fashioned monstrous idols that looked as though they would come to life at any moment.

Frankie led the way, climbing the cracked steps.

Summers was finding it increasingly hard to accept the reality of his situation and his surroundings. Even as someone who had known wealth his entire life, he found himself reflecting that the amount of money that Morgenstein must have spent on this project was astounding. He had just reached the top of the raised platform and was about to cross over to where Frankie and K'teshra were stood when there came a terrible scream from behind him. Spinning round, his heart skipped a beat as he saw five man-like creatures, their skin grey and scaly, come running out of the darkness.

Two of the brutes were armed with stone-bladed clubs.

One of them rushed forward with a weighted javelin and threw it with deadly accuracy at Bridger, catching him squarely in the chest.

With a cry, the elderly man fell.

"Holy shit!" Summers cried. His vision clouded temporarily as everything became a terrible blur; his mind unable and unwilling to fully comprehend what was happening. His legs weakened as a surge of adrenaline played havoc with his senses. Somehow, he managed to raise his shield even as one of the grotesques swung its club at him. Parrying the fierce blow, he felt a jolt of pain lance through his arm.

"Fall back!" Frankie yelled from where she stood.

Now that the initial shock had passed, Summers could see that the being before him was in actuality a woman, her face and body painted and covered with hideous markings. Whether she had been one of the unfortunates that had come here, like him, hoping to experience the enjoyable aspects of larping he could not tell for she had been hideously transformed with cosmetics and ragged clothing.

There was also a mad, feral look in her eyes as she swung out a second time with her club.

Again, Summers blocked the blow. For a moment, he considered hacking out with his sword but held back. He then turned and ran, aghast to see that not far from where he stood, K'teshra had already bludgeoned three of his adversaries to the ground and was continuing to beat their twitching forms. This was insane, he thought. Mindless barbarism.

"In here!" Frankie cried. She stood at the entrance to a doorway within the ruined building.

"For Christ's sake!" Summers screamed. His heart was pounding arhythmically in his chest as though it were about to explode and his limbs were trembling with fear. Rushing forward, he scrambled over a low wall and leapt into the shattered structure even as a hurled spear flew over his shoulder and sparked off a moss-covered column. He could hear K'teshra bellowing his wrath as the 'half-orc' thumped and lay waste to those around him—the meaty, bone-crushing thwacks from his spiked cudgel were sickening to the ear. He looked blankly at the sword in his hand.

"We should be going," K'teshra said as he plodded over, having defeated the attackers. "The troglodytes may soon come back in greater numbers."

Summers was numb. *Troglodytes*—they were people dressed as monsters. And now they were dead. The thoughts that swirled darkly through his mind were filled with terror and pessimism. This place and those in it were designed with one purpose in mind—murder. He had now convinced himself that the sadistic creator of this perverse death-trap was, as his initial brief had stated, watching his every move. No doubt hidden close circuit cameras were cunningly and strategically installed so as to relay images directly to Morgenstein, who, like some sick Roman emperor at the arena, was deriving pleasure from the bloodshed and the suffering. However, that was only one worry—of greater concern was the company he presently shared. Noting the blood spattered on the 'half-orc' only served to confirm the latter's murderous, brutal nature.

"Look, I know things are hard but we—" Frankie started.

"*Hard?*" Summers asked incredulously. He got to his feet. "I can't understand how you still can't see this for what it really is. Are *you* blind or am I mad?" A new thought—that these two, whom, at the end of the day he knew absolutely nothing about, were in some way working with Morgenstein flashed into his mind. If such were the case it explained a lot. Were they 'plants'—actors assigned to his group from the outset to orchestrate this deadly operation? Or was a deep paranoia taking over his rational thinking?

"I'm not doubting that this is a question of survival," Frankie admitted. "In order to do which, we have to keep going. If we give up now, all is lost. Only by staying strong and focused are we going to get through this damnable maze."

"You realise you've killed these people? That you're a murderer?" Summers fixed his gaze on K'teshra.

The 'half-orc' shrugged his shoulders. "In case you didn't notice, *they* attacked me first. What would you have had me do? Roll over like a puppy and let them beat the crap out of me?"

Summers did not know what to do. This was the first time in his life he had ever faced someone as cold-hearted and as uncaring. Was the man psychotic? On drugs? Or just so deeply entrenched in the persona of the character he had been chosen to play that it superseded all moral reasoning—had in effect dehumanised him? And as for Frankie—well he just wasn't sure about her.

From far-off, yet still too close for comfort, came the disturbing sound of echoing wails.

Spiked club in hand, K'teshra walked over to the doorway and looked out.

It was at that moment, whether due to fear, an incipient madness or an urgent desire to escape from the horror of his situation, that a fierce compulsion gripped Summers. Rushing past Frankie, he darted for the exit nearest to him. Deaf to her calls for him to come back, he kept running, his movement hampered by the chain mail armour he wore. The lighting was poor but at least the tunnel was dry and the fact that it sloped sown slightly assisted his going. There were openings to his left and right which he chose to ignore, clinging to the desperate hope that they were but false routes. He soon came to a junction where he decided to go right. After twenty or so yards he then arrived at a crossroads, where, after a moment's indecision, he then went left, soon finding himself in a much smaller cavern from the one he had fled from.

The floor was strewn with rocks. From the ceiling, long, fang-like stalactites hung down threateningly; their constant dripping creating glistening, milky pools on the ground. The sound of the steady plopping echoed eerily; amplified due to the strange, subterranean acoustics.

Summers paused. He was breathing heavily, surprised to see that his exhaled breath was steaming in the cold, dank air.

"Where are you?"

Frankie's shout from somewhere not too far behind him, caused Summers to turn his head. He could see little but the shadowy tunnel he had just come from. Quickly, he made for a darker patch of shadow at the far end of the cavern. He had taken only a few steps when his feet slipped on the mineral secretions and he went sprawling, landing painfully on his left knee. Biting back the pain that jarred through his leg, he pulled himself into the pool of darkness. No sooner had he done so when he heard the sound of approaching footsteps and several seconds later his two former companions stepped into view.

"Do you think he came this way?" K'teshra asked, staring from side to side.

"I don't know," Frankie answered. "Although I thought I heard something."

Summers dared not breathe. Part of his mind was still wrestling with the wisdom of his actions. What exactly did he have to gain from going on alone? Surely there was increased safety in numbers? Still, experience had shown him that these two were far from what he considered ideal team members. And whilst he had no reason, as yet, to distrust them, neither had he any reason to go along with their wanton inability to realise the seriousness of their predicament.

"Stupid bastard isn't going to get far on his own," K'teshra growled.

"Ah, well. Maybe we'll find him further back, down one of those side passages," said Frankie. "Either that or skewered at the bottom of a spiked pit." With a final look around her, she turned and the two of them went back the way they had come.

Alone, in the darkness, Summers waited. Inwardly, he was still debating as to whether or not he had made the right choice in parting company. On the face of it, many would have deemed his actions foolish, for there was no doubt a party was stronger than an individual when it came to survivability—something he knew only too well from his previous larping experiences. But there was something—a sense of *wrongness*—that he had felt about Frankie and K'teshra from the outset. He found himself wondering what, or rather *who*, they were in the real world. Assuming they were genuine larpers and not stooges in the employ of Morgenstein, they were in all probability wealthy, successful people. Maybe they knew each other? Maybe they were related?

Aside from the echoing drips, all was silent.

Exhaling a deep breath, Summers got painfully to his feet. There did not appear to be any other exits from the cavern and so he retraced his steps, paused to check that the others were not in sight and then entered the tunnel. It was then that a sudden thought struck him— assuming his prior companions were in cahoots with Morgenstein, it was conceivable that, once they abandoned looking for him, they would head out. If such were the case, then, providing he could catch up with them, he could surreptitiously follow them out.

* * * *

Summers was well and truly lost. Without a wristwatch or any means of tracking time, he did not know how long he had been wandering these gloomy, menacing passages. It could well have been a couple of hours and all that time he had heard nothing of the others. He came to a pause at a junction—one that looked infuriatingly like the one he had just come from and the one before that. He was thirsty and even though he had eaten a hearty breakfast, he was beginning to feel hungry—a sign, which he interpreted as meaning it was well past lunch. Possessed of a fantastical imagination as he was and well-read in the Classics, he soon found himself likening this place to the Cretan labyrinth in which Theseus had slain the half-man, half-bull monster—the minotaur. Only this time there was no Ariadne nor had he been trailing a ball of string behind him. Futility and despair gnawed at his senses. The strain on his sanity was immense and he knew he could not endure this for much longer. In these long, echoing passages, with only the flickering lantern light, the shadows were huge and fearsome, leaping out at him from all sides, filling the hidden alcoves until he came up to them, with midnight shadows, sending his heart chittering like a frightened animal inside his chest, hammering without pause against his ribs.

It was getting colder.

The passage before him turned at an acute angle and came to a dead end.

"Shit!" Summers cursed. Hopelessness gripped him; enervated him—and for the first time he was fully struck by the realisation that, in all likelihood, he was going to die down here. Aside from the traps and the 'monsters', the other main dangers were dehydration or succumbing to madness. For the best part of a minute, he stared blankly at the wall.

"Warrior from Lyadra! I see you're all alone! Nevertheless, you have progressed far and for that, I salute you!"

Summers stared, wide-eyed, trying to locate the source of the odd, tinny voice. He was certain it had come from numerous directions, an indicator that there was an array of hidden speakers.

"Few have made it this far."

"To Hell with you Morgenstein!" Summers shouted, his rage boiling to the surface. "When I get out of here you're a dead man. Why, even if I don't, you can be sure you're not going to get away with this. Bastard!"

"You are in no position to threaten me."

"You're nothing but a coward! Show yourself—show me what you're made of!" Summers yelled defiantly. "Stop hiding behind your cameras and speakers." He heard a short, barely audible laugh and then nothing. Gritting his teeth, he retraced his steps, taking the first left turn he reached. He walked confidently for the last thing he wanted was to show any signs of weakness—to provide the insane mastermind behind this twisted contrivance that satisfaction.

The tunnel narrowed, the gradient now slightly uphill. The rough, glistening, natural rock walls gave way to carved stone blocks.

This solo adventuring was definitely not for him and as Summers stood there, weighing up his options, he silently cursed himself for leaving the others. With trepidation, he then took several short steps, his grip tight around the hilt of his sword, not knowing what, if anything, might come screaming out of the darkness—some fiendish horror that would rend him limb from limb and no doubt feast on his bloody remains.

Then, with a suddenness that made him jump, a section of the wall just behind him slid to one side, spilling an incongruous electric-white light into the passage.

Two figures emerged from the secret door.

Summers turned and with a huge surge of relief, he recognised Torrence. The other person was a stranger—a dark-haired, athletically built woman he had briefly noticed at breakfast. Both looked weary.

"Chris! Thank God you're alive!" Torrence embraced his friend.

"Am I glad to see you…I thought you were dead." Had the situation not been so perilous Summers would have laughed with joy. The elation at seeing his friend again, something he was unsure he would ever do, sent a deeply emotional sensation through him that almost brought tears to his eyes. Maybe now he had a chance of getting out of this hell-hole. "Hayes?"

"I'm afraid he's gone."

"So could we be if we don't find a way out of here," the woman added. She extended a hand to Summers which he shook. "The name's Abbie."

"Hello, Abbie." Summers nodded. "Do either of you know what the hell's going on, and more importantly—a way out of here and off this bloody island?"

* * * *

Following the maintenance tunnels they eventually found an alternative exit from the dungeon. They had discovered no one else either above or below ground, permitting them to conduct a thorough search for anything of use in escaping. It was Abbie who found the self-assembly hang gliders and suggested using them to get across to the mainland, something which although possible was not without its own risks. Still, having found no boat or means of contacting the outside world it looked the only alternative. At least the winds were favourable.

"It was pandemonium," said Torrence from where he sat putting the framework of his hang glider together atop Tindholmur. "We were being led to one of the outbuildings when I caught a whiff of something downright foul. At first I thought it was some kind of pollution from the sea but when I started to see wisps of grey smoke coming from one of the tall chimneys I grew suspicious. Something just wasn't right...and I couldn't see any of the others."

"I noticed it too," said Abbie. "When I asked our guide what it was he just said they'd had a problem with some of the cooking facilities. Next thing I knew these folk came running towards me; foaming at the mouth, white-eyed and shaking."

"They'd been gassed, of that I've no doubt," Torrence answered. "You could tell just by looking at them. Their skin was all...blotchy, as though they'd been sprayed with a mild acid. Anyway, that was enough for us to turn and run. We went one way and the others in our group went another."

"And Morgenstein?" Summers asked.

"Let the authorities deal with that bastard. First, let's get off this island."

* * * *

Summers watched as his friend ran down the decline. Moments later, he was airborne, the wide span of the red wings of the hang glider uplifted by the strong wind. Like Torrence, he had done this before so having fitted himself into his harness and having done all the precautionary checks, he too set off. With a cry of delight and a rush of adrenaline, the ground disappeared from beneath his feet and he was soaring like an eagle.

It was then he heard the shot.

A moment later, there came a second.

Content with her marksmanship, Abbie Morgenstein began to disassemble her telescopic-sighted rifle.